Negative Image

Parked opposite the door was an orange VW camper streaked with rust. The window was down. Inside was a man with a red beard that spread halfway down his chest. He was holding an automatic, its barrel resting on the sill of the window and its muzzle pointing directly at me.

I glanced up the road. To my relief we weren't alone. A small man was walking towards us. He was young but already going bald. Surely they wouldn't dare do anything in front of witnesses?

Smith swore.

The balding man lifted his right arm. He was carrying a gun too.

NEGATIVE IMAGE

Andrew Taylor

Lions

An Imprint of HarperCollins*Publishers*

First published in in the U.K. in 1992 in Lions
3 5 7 9 8 6 4 2

Lions is an imprint of
HarperCollins Children's Books, a division of
HarperCollins Publishers Ltd,
77–85 Fulham Palace Road,
Hammersmith, London W6 8JB

Printed and bound in Great Britain by
HarperCollins Manufacturing, Glasgow

CHAPTER ONE

The cop was a big man with a fat, flushed face and small, very blue eyes. He wore a strange uniform but a cop's a cop in any language. He took a step towards me.

"And who might you be?" he said.

"Chris Dalham."

My voice sounded normal, and I was pleased about that. I didn't feel normal. This gorilla had jumped out from behind a bush as I turned into the drive.

"Let's see some I.D."

Another guy was coming down the driveway from the house. The evening sun was right behind him: at first he was just a silhouette with a long shadow stretching down the drive towards us. As he drew nearer I saw that he was carrying a walkie-talkie. He wasn't in uniform but he radiated the same gorilla-like aura.

I got my passport out of the backpack. Technically the British don't need passports in Ireland but the travel agent had told me I might find it useful. Too right.

The first cop examined the passport and put his hand out for the backpack. He poked through the contents. The second one just stared at me. He had a little chin, a big nose and one of those permanent smiles that make your flesh crawl.

He started with my hair and worked his way down shirt and jeans to my trainers. Then his eyes travelled back to my hair. He let out his breath in a silent whistle, as if he couldn't believe what he was seeing. People over 25 often feel that way about my hair but usually they don't make it quite so obvious.

Meanwhile his fat friend had found my old Zeiss Ikon.

His thick fingers tugged at the zip of the case. He pulled out the camera.

"Do you want me to open it for you?" I said. The lens of a Zeiss Ikon folds up into the body of the camera.

He tried to force the lens open with his thumbnail. At last I could stand it no longer.

"You press that little button on the top," I said. "No, not that one: the one on the right."

He did as I'd suggested and the lens sprang out. I knew I'd annoyed him. I'd also shown him a way to get even with me. He examined the camera carefully. I guessed what he was going to do.

"Don't open it," I said. "Please."

He found the little catch on the side that released the back. His thumb on the catch, he glanced at me with his piggy eyes: making sure of his audience, I suppose, making sure I knew he was going to ruin a partly-exposed film.

He pressed the catch. The back opened. The camera was empty.

"Was that meant to be a joke?" he said, very softly.

"No," I lied. "It's just that these old cameras are very delicate. I could have opened it for you."

"Whoops," he said.

The Zeiss slipped through his fingers. Without thinking, I lunged at his hand. He stepped back, and the movement probably saved the camera. It landed on grass. It would have landed on gravel. I picked it up.

The plain-clothes cop was still smiling. "And what are you doing here?" he said in a conversational sort of voice.

I put on the innocent expression. "I've come to see Paul Anders." The two men frowned and I added, just to be helpful: "The musician."

"Well, he doesn't live here."

"No, I think he's got a flat in London."

"You're in the wrong city," Cop Number 1 said.

"Wrong country," Cop Number 2 said, with a little giggle.

"He's playing in Dublin tomorrow night," I explained. "That's why I'm here."

"Okay," Number 2 went on. "So that's why you're in Dublin. You got a ticket for this concert?"

"Not yet."

He grunted. "But what we'd like to know is why you're *here*, outside this house."

"I'm coming to stay for a couple of nights. This is eighty-five Bray Road South, isn't it?"

They traded glances. Number 1 said, "Ah. So of course you'll know who lives here?"

He waved his hand at the long, white house behind him. It was a modern, single-storey place in the middle of an acre or two of garden.

"Smith invited me," I said.

"Ah," said Number 2. "Smith is it? Now there's imagination for you."

"A girl called Smith," I went on. "She's about my age—American. But she doesn't live here. She's staying here with her mother. I don't know the owner's name."

This was getting kind of awkward. You see, I couldn't prove a thing. Smith had phoned me a couple of nights ago and asked me over. She said she'd cleared it with her mother and their hosts and gave me the address. It was all done on the telephone. I had nothing in writing.

"Smith?" Number 2 rolled the word around his mouth as if he liked the taste. "Does this girl have another name?"

"Of course she does. But I don't know what it is." Smith's first name is something unpronounceably Polish and she doesn't like using it.

"And her mother? Is she called Smith too? Mrs Smith, maybe?"

"I don't know. Her father's called Drew Smith, but her parents are divorced so her mother may not – "

"Drew Smith. This is progress. Not even *Mister* Smith. Drew Smith. I like it."

Personally I didn't like it one little bit. "He lives in London," I said. "Like Paul Anders. And me, come to that. I – "

"You trying to be smart?" Number 1 interrupted.

"Just helpful."

Number 2 backed away and began to chat to his walkie-talkie. Number 1 took a step past me so he was standing between me and the road. I folded up the camera and put it away. Number 2 wasn't looking at me and Number 1 had the sun in his eyes so I don't think they noticed how my fingers were shaking.

By now the light was just beginning to bleed out of the sky. There was a lot of traffic—familiar cars with unfamiliar numberplates. No one even glanced at me and the cops. I was hot and sweaty after a whole summer day spent cooped up on trains and buses, not to mention the ferry. I was hungry and thirsty. I'd hoped that Smith would meet me at the Ferryport but she hadn't bothered. I'd spent 48 hours thinking about seeing her again, and now she wasn't even here. And now—well, let's be fearlessly frank about this—I was scared.

What the hell was going on? Usually when you hit trouble at least you know what it is. But I had no idea what was happening. To make things worse, I was in a strange land, all the stranger for being so similar to England. Two cops guarding a private house and treating me like a potential housebreaker? It didn't make any kind of sense. Maybe I'd misheard the address. Maybe Smith was playing a hoax on me.

A moment later, a guy in a grey suit came out of the house. He had a tired face and his chin was blue with stubble. He went into a huddle with the chinless wonder. Then he beckoned me over and made me go through the story all over again.

"Okay," he said when I'd finished. He had one of those smooth, soft voices that sound like Guinness would sound if Guinness could talk. "Let me see if I've got it right. This

8

American girl's a friend of yours and she lives in England with her dad. Her mother comes over to Dublin from the States and is staying here with your friend. And the girl asks you over for a concert. You don't know her first name or her mother's name or the name of the people they're staying with. Right?"

"Right," I said. I nodded towards the house. "They must know I'm coming. Can't you ask someone?"

"I would if I could. There's no one at home."

"Look—what is this?"

"I'm afraid you're – "

At that moment a car roared into the driveway and braked sharply. Cop Number 1 swore and jumped backwards just in time to avoid being hit. The other two swung round as though they'd been stung.

"What's going on?" the driver snapped. "Have we had a burglary or something?"

I took an instant dislike to the owner of that voice. I didn't like the fact that I was scared of the police and he wasn't. I didn't like his arrogance. I didn't like his Triumph Spitfire Mark IV—bright red, the top down, in beautiful nick: the perfect summer car. Most of all I didn't like the way he draped his arm along the back of the passenger seat as he waited for an answer.

Smith was sitting in the passenger seat. She was wearing dark glasses. The sun was full on her face. She looked very attractive but somehow remote, like a photo of a model in a glossy magazine.

"Not exactly," said the man in the grey suit. "And who might you be, sir?"

Sir? The driver wasn't much older than me. Why hadn't the cops called me "sir"?

"Gerald Kinahan. I live here. And you?"

The cop produced a warrant card and flashed it at Gerald.

"Well, Inspector?" Gerald shaded his eyes from the sun. "What's the problem?"

"Do you happen to know where your father is, sir?"

"He went out to dinner. To Venger's, I think."

"In Upper Leeson Street?"

Gerald nodded. I looked at Smith. She was looking at Gerald.

"Social, is it?" the Inspector said.

"Why do you want to know?"

"I'll explain later."

Gerald shrugged. "It's a business meeting with one of the directors of Vichy-White-Duloz. I don't know the man's name. My father's there in an advisory capacity—Ms Weyburn asked him to come."

"Who?"

"She's staying with us. She and my father were going to the restaurant straight from work."

"From Biercetown House?"

"You're very well informed."

"Is anyone called Smith staying with you?"

Gerald glanced at his passenger. His hand dropped on to her shoulder.

"This is Smith," he said. "She's Ms Weyburn's daughter."

"And we have someone here who says he's come to stay with you." The Inspector nodded at me and I moved forward, away from the other two cops. "His name's Chris Dalham."

Smith sat up, dislodging Gerald's hand. Those dark glasses made her look older, like a stranger.

"Hi," I said to the Triumph Spitfire. I was doing my best to be friendly.

"So there you are," Gerald Kinahan said. "Where the hell have you been?"

CHAPTER TWO

"Fearlessly Frank" is the title of a track on *Negative Image*, which is the most recent Paul Anders album. Not many people know that. Paul Anders is a minority taste.

Smith kicked off her sandals and curled up in an armchair. She was wearing a baggy tee-shirt and shorts. "You know what your trouble is?" she said. "You got a negative image of yourself. That's why you had to make the gardai mad. What's the point of it?"

I guessed the gardai were the Irish police. "I didn't mean to make them mad," I said. "I was just being fearlessly frank. You know me."

I was trying to make a joke out of it. I'd given her a tape I'd made of the album and I knew she liked it. Or so she said.

"Stop acting so dumb," she said. "We're guests here. We got to think of the Kinahans."

"And your mother, of course," I suggested, which was a little nasty of me. This house was making me nervous.

"Astrid? You can leave her out of it, okay?"

Smith cracked open her second can of lager and reached for an apple. I stuffed my mouth with bread and cheese. For a while we had one of those uncomfortable silences which are really just quarrels without words. It was my fault, at least in part. I knew I shouldn't have mentioned Smith's mother.

We were sitting in a big living room at the back of the Kinahans' house. The room smelled of wood smoke and leather. French windows looked across a terrace and down a long, sloping lawn. Outside it was practically dark. The cops were still around—the Inspector was talking to Gerald in another room and the other two were outside. We still hadn't worked out what they were doing.

I glanced at the big, expensively-framed colour photographs on the walls: mainly street scenes and architectural details. Someone had too much money and too little talent.

"How's your dad?" I said, just to break the silence.

Smith shrugged. "He's working. Same old story."

The silence returned. Drew Smith got himself roughed up last month—physically, I mean—and then he had a dose of what you might call girlfriend trouble. Smith's parents are a couple of emotional disaster areas.

"If you must know," Smith went on, "he's licking his wounds. That's one reason I'm here."

"Come again?"

"Astrid called on Sunday, said she was going to be in Dublin for a few days and would I like to come over. I said yes. Anything seemed better than staying with my father."

"I thought you hadn't seen your mother for years."

I topped up Smith's glass and waited.

"I haven't. She's been too busy making money."

"So why the change of policy?"

Smith looked at me. She's got astonishing blue eyes with sort of greeny flecks in them.

"How do I know? Maybe she's feeling guilty. Maybe it's because she's in love with Kinahan."

"With *Gerald?*"

"Gerald's father—Stephen. He's a widower . . . He and Mom went through Harvard Business School together. The way I figure it, she's trying to show him that she's not all career and no family. I'm living proof that she's a three-dimensional woman."

"Take it easy," I said.

"This evening," Smith went on, "she proved what really matters to her. Vichy-White-Duloz want to buy her company. She's turned them down. Or at least that's

12

what she said she was going to do. You know what she said last night? 'It'd be like selling my soul.'"

"It's her life."

"Yeah, and it's my life too. I wish she'd remember that. Parents. Who needs them?"

She was near to tears.

"Who's this creep Gerald?" I said.

As I'd hoped, the question made her angry and prevented her from crying.

"He's not a creep," she yelled at me. "And he's a damn sight more mature than some people I could name."

"Did he take these photos?" I asked. I waved my hand at the pretty pictures on the wall.

She nodded.

"I see."

"And what's that supposed to mean?" Smith said.

I changed tack. "What happened this evening? Did you and Gerald go to meet me at the Ferryport?'

She glared at me. "Of course we did. And you weren't there."

"I didn't see you either."

It turned out that Smith and Gerald had got there just after the ferry docked. I had been one of the first foot-passengers off the boat. We must have missed each other by seconds. Smith said I should have waited—I should have known she would be there. I pointed out that unfortunately I wasn't telepathic.

Smith poked her chin in the air. "If you'd come by air, none of this would have happened."

We nearly had another quarrel. When she'd phoned on Wednesday night to say Paul Anders was doing a gig in Dublin on Saturday and would I like to come, she offered to pay my air fare. This is one of our problems. Smith may be low on parental affection but she's never short of money.

I'd said no, of course. Normally that would have been that: no Dublin, no Paul Anders and no Smith. But I'd just won £100, the third prize in a photographic competition.

13

I'd been planning to spend it on a second-hand camera or maybe an enlarger. I wanted those things badly. I wanted to see Smith even more. On my own terms.

On the way back from the Ferryport, she told me, the Spitfire had broken down. Gerald had fixed it—Smith implied that Gerald was the sort of bloke who could effortlessly fix anything—but neither of them was in the best of tempers when they got back to Bray Road South.

"And then we had to deal with the cops," Smith said.

"Ah yes," I said. "And what are they doing here?"

"How do I know?"

"It sounded like they wanted Mr Kinahan. What's he done?"

She frowned. "But it wasn't like that, was it? I didn't get the impression they were trying to bust him. It was more like they were worried about him."

"What does he do?"

"He's got a research laboratory somewhere south of Dublin. Gerald's his personal assistant."

"Jobs for the boys," I said, and my voice sounded sour. I was thinking of the Spitfire and all that fancy photographic equipment.

Smith opened her mouth to blast me out. Before she had had time to speak, a car roared up the drive. Somewhere in the house a dog began to bark. Doors slammed.

No one came into the living room. I wondered if they had forgotten about us. All this uncertainty—the cops on one side and Gerald Kinahan on the other—was making me jumpy. I tried to cheer myself up with the thought that, whatever happened, I was going to see Paul Anders.

"So you got the tickets, then?"

Smith looked blankly at me. Then she dragged her mind back from wherever it had been and said, "Oh, you mean Paul Anders? We'll have to pick them up tomorrow. I tried to get them yesterday but the—what's *that?*"

So she was feeling jumpy too. I listened. *Scrape-scrape-scrape*, faint but getting louder.

"It's coming from the door," I said.

Smith leapt up and opened it. A little dog bounded into the room. He licked Smith's hand and then bounced across to me. I didn't know what breed he was, if any—he was black and brown and white, with floppy ears and a very wet tongue. He rolled on his back and put his legs in the air. I scratched his belly. It was nice that someone in this country was unconditionally pleased to see me.

"His name's Robby," Smith said.

There were voices in the hall. The Inspector was saying, "Better safe than sorry, Mr Kinahan. Better safe than sorry."

Suddenly the room seemed full of people—a small, slim woman with jet-black hair, Gerald Kinahan and an older man with a rumpled face who had to be his father.

Robby and I scrambled off the floor. I don't know about Robby but I felt rather stupid. The dog rushed over to Stephen Kinahan and tried to climb up his trouser leg.

There was a flurry of introductions. Astrid Weyburn was one of those glossy people who seem to belong to another, higher species. She looked not so much at me as through me as she shook my hand: it was as though her eyes were focused on a point six inches behind the back of my skull.

"Hi, Chris," she said, lowering and refocusing her eyes so she could examine the blob of tomato ketchup on my shirt. "Ah—Smith's told us *so* much about you."

Oh God, I thought: here we go again. I often have this effect on my friends' parents.

But not on Stephen Kinahan. He said he was pleased to meet me, and he said it as if he really meant it. He apologized for all the confusion and asked if I'd had a proper meal. Meanwhile Astrid Weyburn was looking at the empty lager cans on the coffee table. Her lips flickered out of shape as if she had unexpectedly taken a bite of lemon.

Gerald sidled over to Smith and said something in such a low voice that I couldn't hear it. But I saw Smith's smile.

15

Kinahan turned back to Astrid, back to a conversation they must have been having beforehand. "I really think the three of you should move to a hotel. Just in case, eh?"

"Ah no." She waggled her finger. "You're not going to get rid of us that easily, Stephen."

"It'd be safer."

"Be rational. You told the police they were overreacting. And now you're asking *me* to overreact too."

"It's not that I want you to go." Their eyes met, and he seemed to remember that he and Astrid weren't alone in the room. He scratched Robby's head and added hastily, "Any of you, that is."

"Forewarned is forearmed. We've got a twenty-four-hour guard. So what's the problem?"

"But I'd never forgive myself if something happened."

"It won't. You heard what the guy said. They're just cranks, Stephen, and this is Ireland, not England or the States. We'll take sensible precautions, fine, but let's not get paranoid about this."

She batted her eyelids at him and the argument was over. Kinahan looked at Astrid the way Robby was looking at him. My God, it's an indecent sight: the middle-aged in love.

An awkward silence settled over the room.

Then Smith spoke—in that calm little voice of hers that means she's seething inside: "Would someone *please* tell me what's happening?"

Stephen Kinahan cleared his throat. "The gardai had a tip-off from the British police. It seems I've been targeted by an English animal rights group." He shrugged. "The gardai think I should take it seriously."

"Targeted?" Smith said.

The room was very still. Robby whined softly and nudged Kinahan's hand with his nose. Kinahan stroked the dog's head. The man didn't look scared: just embarrassed.

"Yes," he said at last. "Targeted. They plan to kill me."

16

CHAPTER THREE

The next day was Saturday. My old friend the chinless wonder came to breakfast. That wasn't the cop's main reason for being there. He'd come to show Stephen Kinahan how to check his mail before he opened it and his car before he started it.

Just in case someone wanted Stephen Kinahan to go to work on a bomb.

The chinless wonder was the life and soul of the party. Maybe he liked having an audience. "Call me Patrick," he said. "After all, we'll probably be seeing quite a lot of one another."

Kinahan decided that the whole household had better hear the lecture. Just in case.

"If it's PAF," Patrick said, "and our latest information is that it most likely is, they'll probably go for PE4."

We looked blankly at him. He sipped his coffee.

"PAF: the People for Animals Faction. They're a splinter group from the Animal Liberation Front: very nasty, very activist. They organized into cells right from the start, which means they're also very difficult to penetrate. They did that job at Manchester University last month. You remember? They got the secretary rather than the professor himself. That was PE4 used in conjunction with a mercury tilt trigger."

"PE4's an explosive, then?" Kinahan sounded very calm. He'd cut himself shaving. In his position my hands would have been shaking too.

Patrick nodded. "Made by the Royal Ordnance, no less. Strictly for military use. God knows how they got it. The Brits think PAF must be getting help from outside. Still." He beamed at us. "We've got one advantage, haven't we?

17

If they come here, they'll be playing away for the first time. That'll make it much harder for them."

He sounded like a manager giving his team a pep talk before the big match. He talked about mercury tilt triggers and the importance of watching your rearview mirror. He reckoned that only Stephen Kinahan was in danger: after getting the wrong person at Manchester, PAF wouldn't want to make the same mistake again. But the rest of us had to keep our eyes open.

"It's just like the CIA motto says." Patrick looked at Astrid. "'Eternal vigilance is the price of peace.' Or is that someone else's motto?"

After breakfast, we split up. Patrick, Astrid and Stephen Kinahan were going down to Biercetown House, where the research laboratory was, to check security procedures. Gerald had offered to drive Smith and me into central Dublin to buy the tickets and have a look round. The gardai would keep the house under surveillance in our absence.

Gerald made this big deal of checking underneath the Spitfire for bombs before we set off. The car had been locked in the garage all night, along with Stephen's Volvo.

Triumph Spitfires are lovely little motors but they do have one drawback: they're designed for two people not three. Smith sat beside Gerald, and I squeezed into the space behind the seats. If I'd been a suitcase I would have been very comfortable.

No one talked much because we had the hood down. At first I spent the time looking at the back of Gerald's neck and wishing that looks could kill. He didn't have much that I didn't have too. Just a job and a car and an unlimited amount to spend on clothes. He was a year or two older and maybe an inch taller. In my personal opinion he was totally unattractive. But I have to admit I was a little prejudiced.

The traffic got heavier as we neared the centre of the city. We stopped at some traffic lights.

18

Smith said to Gerald, "I didn't realize you had an animal house at Biercetown."

The back of his neck turned pink. "It's quite a small one. We've got the strictest humanitarian controls. You should talk to my father about it."

"You keep very quiet about it."

His hands tightened on the steering wheel. "These days you have to. Can you blame us, with people like PAF around?"

"I'm thinking about becoming a vegetarian," Smith said.

"Me too." A bead of sweat appeared on Gerald's neck. It trapped a bit of sunshine and twinkled at me. "You know your mother is . . . ?"

"What about her?"

"I assumed you'd know—she's one of our clients, as well as a friend of Dad's. She's hoping to launch a new cosmetic range for the European market. We're running tests on the products."

"No,' Smith said. "I didn't know."

The lights changed from red to green and Gerald let out the clutch too sharply. The car jerked away. They stopped talking and I looked at Dublin instead.

The city took me by surprise. I suppose my subconscious had been expecting picturesque peasants drinking Guinness by the gallon and maybe the occasional leprechaun and a few donkeys munching four-leafed clovers. But apart from the green pillar boxes and a few other details, Dublin was just like parts of London or Bristol or Birmingham—the same sort of people in the same sort of clothes, the same seedy buildings and the same posters advertising the same films and concerts. And while I looked at Dublin I was wondering exactly what "running tests on the products" entailed. Smothering monkeys with mascara? Coating white mice with nail varnish? It seemed one hell of a way to make a living.

Gerald found a slot for the Spitfire in a car park north of St Stephen's Green. The three of us threaded our way through a maze of streets to buy the tickets. You can't walk three abreast along crowded pavements. Smith and Gerald went in front, not quite touching, while I trailed behind feeling like a two-legged gooseberry.

Things improved at the ticket agency. Smith and Gerald went up to the counter. I distinctly heard Smith asking for two seats. Not three: it could only mean that Gerald wasn't coming.

When we got outside I paid Smith what I owed her for my ticket.

"There was really no need to get them in advance," Gerald said in that superior voice of his. "You can always get tickets at the door at the Warehouse. They never play to capacity."

"I'm not taking any chances," I said. "Not this time."

I'd been trying to see Paul Anders for nearly a year. Smith and I nearly made it last month—he was playing in London, at the Willesden Palace. We even had the tickets. But something came up. That, as they say, is another story.

"They only have minor bands, you see," Gerald went on, "and the Warehouse is in the middle of nowhere."

"Is that why you aren't coming?" I asked.

"Well, no. I'd have liked to come with you . . . both." Gerald glanced at Smith and she gave him a smile. "Thing is, I've got something else lined up."

It wasn't what he'd said, it was the way he'd glanced at Smith: they had a little secret and they were keeping me out of it.

"What a shame," I said cheerfully. "How are we going to spend the day?"

"It's up to you," Gerald said.

"I want to buy some jeans," Smith said. "Then maybe a bit of sightseeing. I expect Chris will want to take a few photos."

Gerald looked at the Zeiss Ikon and raised his eyebrows. "Oh, is that a camera?"

Snide. Very snide. I nodded, not trusting myself to speak.

He turned back to Smith. "Anyway, why don't we separate now and meet up for lunch? I want to do a bit of shopping too. We could meet at the Café Swann on Dawson Street. It's probably the best place in town for vegetarian food."

It ended up with their going one way and my going the other. Gerald had offered to show Smith where a particular shop was; it was on his way—no problem. Like hell, I thought.

I really didn't want to follow them. It made me feel sneaky and mean. I'd never felt like this before and I hope I never feel like it again. I didn't own Smith any more than she owned me. Even then I knew I was on a hiding to nothing. If my suspicions were right, I'd feel even worse. And if they were wrong, I'd still feel even worse.

There was nothing I could do about it except open up the camera and walk with it in my hand. Not much of an excuse if they bumped into me but slightly better than nothing. "Fancy seeing you here," I would say. "I was just going to take a photo of . . . " whatever was in front of the lens.

Smith and Gerald didn't look back. At first it was easy enough to keep them in sight. They weren't holding hands or anything. But they were talking as they walked and their heads were very close together. They looked like a couple. We passed shop after shop that sold jeans.

Then they turned into an alley, left into a side street and cut across an open space in front of a big grey church. It was harder to follow them: there was less cover. I had to drop back, which meant I increased the chance of losing them.

That was how I came to notice the man in the green shirt.

I'd registered the sight of him before. He was just odd enough to stand out from the crowd—plump, with baggy

21

white trousers and very narrow shoulders. There were damp patches under his armpits. His face was chalky white except for the nose, which had caught the sun. He looked a little like an off-duty circus clown.

Gerald and Smith turned right and disappeared round the end of the church. The man in the green shirt followed. In a way he was doing me a favour. According to Patrick and possibly the CIA, eternal vigilance was the price of peace. So I had a reason to follow Smith and Chris: I was just being vigilant, like the policeman said.

At this stage, of course, I didn't really think the man was following them. I was playing a game with myself. The bloke was probably taking the same zigzagging shortcut across the city as Gerald was. People have their secret ways across their own cities, ways that tourists rarely find.

Two rights and three lefts later, Mr Greenshirt was still on their tail. Then I lost sight of all three of them. I almost ran round the next corner. Gerald and Smith were only about twenty yards away from me. Gerald was pointing at a shopfront. Greenshirt was further down the road, looking in another window.

I darted back. A few seconds later I peered round the corner. Gerald and Smith had vanished—presumably into the shop; there was nowhere else for them to go. And Greenshirt was strolling back towards me.

That was the moment when I stopped pretending to be vigilant and started to feel really worried.

I crossed the road and walked along the opposite pavement. The shop was called Jean Themes. By now, Greenshirt was hovering outside. He had a camera, a Polaroid, slung on his shoulder. He was studying what looked like a map.

The Polaroid and the map implied he was a stranger in Dublin. But surely a stranger wouldn't have zigzagged across the city as confidently as he had done? He hadn't hesitated once. Unless, of course, the stranger was following someone who *did* know the city.

People with cameras are tourists who take photos. I unslung the Zeiss and unfolded the lens. I'd already set the aperture and exposure-time to settings that could cope with the sunlight. I had to guess the distance—it would have made it too obvious if I pointed the camera at Greenshirt and tried to get him into focus.

First I took a shot of an old house a few doors along from the shop: delicate iron railings, concrete blocks where the ground-floor windows used to be; a fanlight above the door; and a spray-gunned BRITS OUT across the door panels. I wound the film on and panned the camera a few degrees to the right. A couple of cars and a van went by, blocking my view. When the road was clear, I pressed the shutter on the man in the green shirt.

My fingers trembled as I shut the camera. I sneaked a glance across the road. Nothing had changed: Smith and Gerald were still inside the shop; the man in the greenshirt was still studying his map. I sauntered back to the corner and turned into a one-way street with grimy old flats on one side and a building site on the other.

What happened next was totally unexpected. A distant road drill and the noise of the traffic masked other sounds. I was wondering whether I should give the undeveloped film straight to the gardai or ask Gerald if he had a darkroom. There were no pedestrians—the only people in sight were a group of kids who had got through the chain-mesh fence that guarded the site and were playing football there.

The blow fell on my shoulder. I let out a yell and collided with a wall. The pain was so intense I thought my collarbone must be broken. I caught a whiff of sour sweat. The Zeiss was wrenched out of my hand.

"Hey!" I yelled. "That's my camera!"

All right, it was a stupid thing to say: a waste of breath. The man in the green shirt sprinted up the street. He ran like a dog swims—clumsily, as though he were out of his usual element—but he covered the ground at quite a lick.

23

No one else had noticed a thing. Cars continued to flow past me. The kids were yelling at one of their number who had just scored an own goal.

I broke into a run. The pain from the shoulder slowed me down. I wasn't playing heroes. I just wanted my camera back. Losing it was like losing an arm or a leg.

The road ended in a shapeless traffic junction. The lights were on the blink and the traffic from half a dozen streets was getting seriously entangled. Yet another church reared up on the corner diagonally across from where I was standing; it was separated from me by a couple of crash barriers and several lanes of stationary cars and lorries. I glimpsed what might have been a green shirt flickering among the dusty bushes in the churchyard.

Then the traffic began to move.

By the time I got across the junction, the man in the green shirt had gone. He wasn't in the churchyard and he wasn't in the church. He wasn't in any of the litterbins either, and nor was my camera.

CHAPTER FOUR

"You were *following* us?" Gerald said. He looked down his nose at me. It was one of those long, straight noses that are ideal for sneering with.

"No, of course not," I said, hoping I didn't look as pink as I felt. "I just happened to catch sight of you. And this man in the green shirt was there—and *he* seemed to be following you."

"Oh, I see. Dogging our footsteps with a magnifying glass, eh? Is that what made you suspicious?"

Gerald grinned at his own wit. He looked across the table at Smith, inviting her to share the joke.

"Go on, Chris," she said, looking at me.

"He was still behind you when you got to Jean Themes. He hung around near the shop while you were inside. That's when I took the photo of him. Next thing I knew, he'd snatched the camera and belted off. I chased after him but it was no use. By the time I got back to the shop you'd gone."

My shoulder was still throbbing but I didn't mention the fact that he had hit me. It would have made it seem as if I wanted their sympathy.

Gerald gave an elaborate shrug. "Look, Chris: this is Dublin in August. Cameras and bags are getting snatched every minute of the day. I mean, count your blessings—you're lucky it wasn't a *good* camera."

I hung onto my temper. I could have pointed out that anyone who's got a low opinion of Zeiss Ikons doesn't know much about photography. Instead I leaned back in my chair and said as calmly as I could, "Don't you think there's just a possibility that the man might have had something to do with PAF? You've just had a

25

warning about them. And it was you he seemed to be interested in."

"'Seemed'—that's the point. We've only got your opinion for that. Even if he was following us, he was probably just after Smith's bag. And when we went into a shop he looked around for something easier—and saw you sauntering along, twirling your camera."

I had to hand it to Gerald. He had a way with words. He had a real talent for putting the boot in: not just that, he did it in a jokey way so you couldn't really object to it. I couldn't work out why he was playing this down so much. To show Smith how brave he was? Or show her what a wimp I was? Or did he really believe that a random mugger had stolen my camera?

"In any case," he said, "why should anyone tail me in the middle of Dublin on a Saturday morning? It's my father they'd want, not me. And if they're planning something they wouldn't do it on the spur of the moment in broad daylight, with dozens of witnesses around."

Smith stared at her lap. We were sitting in the Café Swann, which was in a cool basement with unplastered brick walls. I had arrived late—Dublin is a great city for getting lost in—and Smith and Gerald had already bought lunch. They were having lentil-burgers in granary rolls with a green salad between them. I had a craving for a bacon butty.

"So what do you think we should do?" Smith said to her lap.

"Have you reported it to the police yet?" Gerald asked, managing to imply, oh so subtly, that if I hadn't I needed my head examined.

"No." I'd wanted to talk it over with Smith and Gerald before I went to the cops.

Gerald clicked his tongue in an absent-minded sort of way. "Are you insured?"

I shook my head.

"Hardly worth the bother, I suppose." He heaved a

26

sigh. "If we do report it, it's going to take up half the afternoon."

"I'm sorry about that," I said. "But at least it's my afternoon we're talking about, not yours."

So we all had a ruined afternoon.

Smith said she would come with me to the gardai, so of course Gerald had to come too. I gave them a description of the man, and we told them about the PAF business.

The cops were very thorough and very polite, but I could tell that they thought it was a random mugging too. I didn't think they'd waste too much time scouring the streets of Dublin for off-duty clowns in green shirts.

Mentally I kissed goodbye to the Zeiss Ikon. I knew there would be other, better cameras. I also knew that I'd never feel quite the same about them as I had about the Zeiss.

None of us had much appetite for sightseeing. Gerald kept looking at his watch to show how much time I'd made them waste with the gardai. I was feeling depressed. As for Smith, she was still wrapped in her own thoughts and she gave the impression that she didn't care what we did. If we'd been alone I would have tried to find out what was on her mind—usually there's a good reason for one of her moods—but I couldn't do that with Gerald breathing down her neck.

So we trailed back to the Spitfire. Gerald drove us back to the long white house on Bray Road South.

Astrid and Stephen Kinahan were having tea and scones on a lawn the size of a football field. Robby was panting under Stephen's chair. They'd heard about the mugging, of course—the gardai had relayed the news to Patrick and his boss.

After the first scone, Smith let rip.

I'd known it was coming: I'd recognized the signs. She's not normally a big-mouthed person but occasionally she gets worked up. Then the emotions boil up inside her and spurt out. At different times today I had invented different reasons for her mood: maybe she was in a passionate trance because of Gerald; or she was working up the courage to say that she wanted to finish with me; or seeing her mother was getting her down. As it happens, I was wrong on all counts.

"Excuse me," she said to Stephen in a gabble, "I want to ask you something. I don't mean to be rude, I really want to know: do you make your living by experimenting on animals?"

"Smith!" Astrid squawked.

"No, that's okay," Stephen Kinahan said, his eyes on Smith. "It's a fair question. Yes, I have a research laboratory, and yes, it includes a small animal house. But we believe in reducing the numbers of animals used to the absolute minimum. If we can, we find replacements for animal-based techniques. And we always try to refine the techniques so they cause as little pain and discomfort as possible. Our animals have got a better standard of living than a lot of humans have."

He spoke so slickly that I guessed he'd said all this many times before. I stared at the grass. Gerald helped himself to another scone.

"I still think it's immoral," Smith said. "What right have we got to harm other animals? What makes us so great?"

"That's not the point," Kinahan said calmly. "Suppose I'm out in the jungle and I meet a man-eating tiger that's starving to death. Suppose the tiger eats me. Has the tiger a right to eat me? Of course not. But you can't blame it, can you, any more than you can blame me for not wanting to be eaten. Now look at it the other way. Humans die in all sorts of potentially avoidable ways. Cancer, in childbirth, in surgery—you name it. You can't blame us for trying to avoid those deaths. You could even say we've a duty to try. Over ninety per cent of our work involving animals comes under the heading of medical research. And the purpose of that is quite simply to save lives."

"And make profits for pharmaceutical companies. What about the other ten percent?" Smith glanced at her mother. "What about cosmetics?"

Astrid said, "Can we *please* change the subject?"

Stephen gave her a smile. "In a moment." He turned back to Smith. "You're wearing make-up, I think?"

"So? It's cruelty-free."

"That's how they market it. But it doesn't mean that animals have never been used in testing the ingredients that go into the product. It just means that the manufacturers use ingredients that have already been tested. They're passing the buck. And so, in a way, are you."

Like Gerald, Stephen Kinahan had a way with words. I didn't think he was was being fair to Smith and I wished I could do something to help her.

"I think that's enough for now, Smith," Astrid said. "Remember that Stephen's our host."

Smith turned on her mother. "Why are you running the tests in Ireland? Because the controls on using animals are tougher in the States?"

"I really think that's my affair."

"You've got to look at this in context," Stephen said. "In British laboratories they get through something like thirteen thousand dogs a year. Beagles, mainly. But the RSPCA has to put down around a thousand dogs a day. Unwanted pets. It's tragic, isn't it? At least our dogs live in comfort and die to some purpose."

"Two wrongs don't make a right," I said before I could stop myself.

They all looked at me. Robby wriggled out from under the chair. Stephen tugged his ears and the dog looked adoringly at him. I suddenly realized what breed Robby belonged to.

"He's a beagle, isn't he?" Smith said in a whisper. "You brought him back from your animal house."

Stephen nodded.

Smith said, "Excuse me." She stood up and walked into the house.

That evening we ate early because of the Paul Anders concert. Astrid had cooked some sort of casserole—an old Tennessee recipe, apparently, which involved pork and beans and a lot of things I couldn't identify.

It smelled good and it tasted good. I was starving because I'd only had time to snatch a takeaway sandwich from the Café Swann. So I had three helpings of the Tennessee casserole. There was plenty available because Smith and Gerald just had bread and cheese and salad.

"What is this?" Astrid asked Smith. "Have you gone on a diet or something?"

"I'm a vegetarian," Smith said.

"Since when?"

She shrugged. "I finally made up my mind last night."

"You might have told me."

"Sorry."

What with one thing and another it was not a comfortable meal. The carnivores were at one end of the table and the vegetarians at the other. Afterwards, Gerald phoned for a taxi to take Smith and me to the Warehouse.

"How will you get back?" Stephen asked.

"It's okay—I'm going to meet them," Gerald said.

I glanced at Smith. It was the first I'd heard of the arrangement.

"There's a bar opposite the main entrance," Gerald said to Smith. "I'll wait for you there."

"Don't worry if you can't make it," Smith said. "We can get a cab."

"Oh, I'll be there, all right" Gerald said. And he gave her one of his oily smiles.

The cop on the gate had been warned to expect the taxi. It rolled up to the front door. Gerald practically handed Smith into the back; it was as though he'd been taking lessons in how to treat visiting royalty. I noticed that Smith didn't object. I got in beside her and showed my independence by shutting my own door.

The driver said, "The Warehouse, is it?" and roared off down the drive. He was listening to a match on the radio so we didn't have to talk to him.

"Are you okay?" I said softly.

"Yeah."

That was not exactly informative. I reminded myself that my coming here was Smith's idea. Maybe I had a right to a few answers.

"Why isn't our Gerald coming?" I asked.

"He's got something else on."

"Official Secret, is it?"

Smith shrugged. "If you must know, he's got a date."

"With a girlfriend, you mean?"

I spoke as casually as I could. I doubt if she was fooled. She must have known what I hoped the answer would be. Smith's a lot of things, but she isn't a fool.

"Yes and no," she said at last.

"Does that mean you don't know?"

The driver clapped his hands on the steering wheel. "They've done it! They've done it!" he said. The car veered towards the other side of the road. "Oh no they haven't. The fools. Oh Mother of God!" He turned up the radio even higher.

"It means," Smith said slowly, "that she thinks she's his girlfriend, but after she's seen him tonight she'll know that she isn't. Like I said: yes and no."

We went the rest of the way in silence.

The Warehouse fronted on a main road, with smaller roads running down the sides. It was a tatty building, ripe for demolition—the sort of place you'd expect to have a leaky tin roof and a cracked concrete floor. I wondered what the acoustics were like.

I desperately wanted this concert to be good. Paul

Anders was my discovery and I'd more or less forced his music down Smith's throat. She said she liked him but sometimes I thought she was only saying it to humour me.

The omens were good. There was a queue at the door, and it stretched halfway down one of the side roads. The Irish, I thought, are obviously a nation with taste.

I paid off the taxi while Smith was still searching in her bag for her wallet. We crossed the road and began to work our way through the crowd around the doors. The little foyer was solid with people. Folk-rock blasted out of a couple of speakers mounted on the ceiling. A couple of heavyweight guys in Warehouse tee-shirts were checking tickets at another set of doors directly opposite us.

"Message from Mr Kinahan!"

The shouted words just penetrated the noise barrier. Smith and I stopped, trying to figure out where they had come from. A woman in jeans and a Warehouse tee-shirt elbowed her way towards us. She had lank brown hair and a freckled, earnest face.

"Message from Mr Kinahan," she shouted to me from about three feet away.

"What is it?" Smith said eagerly.

Which Kinahan? Stephen or Gerald?

The woman jerked her head in the direction we'd come. "We'd better go outside," she mouthed.

We struggled back to the street.

"It was a phone call," she said. "The guy said it was urgent and – "

"How did you know it was us?" I said.

"He said you'd be coming in a taxi. Come on."

We followed her along the frontage of the building.

"There's a phone in the office," the woman said over her shoulder. "The side door's round here. I think they said someone's hurt."

She was walking fast, almost running, and her urgency infected Smith and me. She took us into the side road on the left—not the one with the queue. On our right was the high brick wall of the Warehouse and on our left was a row of parked cars. It was still light. I could hear the thud of the music blending with the roar of traffic on the main road.

"It's just down here," she said.

We reached a grubby green door set in the brick wall. The woman held back, allowing us to go first. I twisted the handle and pushed. The door wouldn't budge.

"It's locked or jammed," I said.

As I turned back to them, Smith sucked in her breath.

The woman had moved maybe five yards down the pavement. She was staring at us with a sort of horrified amazement—as if we were freaks in a funfair or something: as if we weren't quite human.

Smith touched my arm. "Look," she said quietly.

Parked opposite the door was an orange VW camper streaked with rust. The window was down. Inside was a man with a red beard that spread halfway down his chest. He was holding an automatic, its barrel resting on the sill of the window and its muzzle pointing directly at me.

I glanced up the road. To my relief we weren't alone. A small man was walking towards us. He was young but already going bald. Surely they wouldn't dare do anything in front of witnesses?

Smith swore.

The balding man lifted his right arm. He was carrying a gun too.

"Okay, Kinahan," the man in the VW said. He beamed all over his fat face. "You've had a change of plan. Hop in."

CHAPTER FIVE

Pretending to be a suitcase in the back of a Triumph Spitfire had not given me a very good opinion of Irish roads.

In Dublin today I'd felt every bump and every pothole all over my body. I remember actually thinking that there couldn't be a worse way to travel. I was wrong.

This time I couldn't reasonably blame either Gerald or Irish road surfaces. Smith and I were lying side by side on the floor of the VW camper. There wasn't much room so at least fifty per cent of Smith was on top of me. We had parcel tape wound round our ankles and wrists. I don't know what Smith had in her mouth but I had what tasted like an old sock.

I suppose it could have been worse. The man who was bald on top had wanted to use parcel tape as a blindfold but the other guy said it would be simpler just to chuck a blanket over us.

"You drive, Julia," the man with the beard said. "Eddy and I will ride in the back."

Unlike the woman, who sounded Irish, he had an English accent—Yorkshire, I think; somewhere up north. Eddy—the one who'd suggested parcel tape as a blindfold—was also English: judging by his voice he could have come from the house next door to mine.

We drove for what seemed like hours. It was all stop-start stuff, with a lot of gear changes: I guessed we were still in Dublin.

"What the hell are you doing?" Eddy said. He was using my head as a footstool.

"I can't find the N11," Julia said.

"What do you mean you can't find it?"

"They stopped signposting it a while back." She sounded

desperate. "There were lots of signs until we reached St. Stephen's Green."

"Hell, I thought you knew this city."

"You thought wrong."

"Hey, you two," the man with the beard said. "These walls have ears. Mind what you say."

Eddy laughed, and it wasn't a pleasant sound. "But it doesn't matter, Finch, does it?"

After that they drove in silence. I had a lot to think about—like how to avoid being car sick; I didn't fancy choking to death on my own vomit. My body was turning into one huge bruise.

Why had they let us hear their names? I could think of two explanations: either Eddy, Finch and Julia weren't their real names or they knew that we would never be in a position where we could pass those names on to the police. On the other hand, maybe that was what Eddy meant us to think: that little snatch of conversation might have been part of a softening-up process.

For what purpose? These people had to be part of the People for Animals Faction. But Smith and I had nothing to do with the research laboratory. Then I remembered that Finch had called me "Kinahan". In all the racket at the Warehouse, Julia might even have said "Message *for* Mr Kinahan", not "*from* Mr Kinahan". The more I thought about it, the more likely it seemed: they thought I was Gerald, and as Smith was there they brought her along for the ride. I wondered if Stephen Kinahan would be kind enough to pay a ransom for me.

By now the camper had picked up speed. I was getting shooting pains in my arms and legs. Smith stirred on top of me. We couldn't even see each other, let alone talk.

"I missed the turning," Julia said, shouting to make herself heard over the noise of the engine. "The map must be wrong."

"Women." Eddy sniffed. "Can't even read a map. Give it here."

I began to get angry at their incompetence. Stupid of me, wasn't it? But the longer they kept us travelling in the camper, the worse it was for me and Smith.

That started me on another line of thought. There had been nothing incompetent about the way they'd kidnapped us. I wondered if they had tailed us to the Warehouse from Bray Road South. No, that wouldn't work—Julia was wearing a Warehouse tee-shirt, so they must have already known we were going to the Paul Anders concert. The tee-shirt was a clever touch. I'd just assumed she was some kind of employee.

"This map doesn't make sense," Eddy said.

"Told you so," Julia snapped.

"Typical Irish. Can't even draw a map."

"We do it intentionally," Julia said. "Just to confuse the Brits if they try to invade us again."

Julia's tee-shirt meant they must have had time to plan the whole thing carefully. I thought about the man in the green shirt. I'd only noticed him after Smith and Gerald went off by themselves. But he might have been following us earlier in the morning, when we went to the ticket agency. He could have been behind Gerald and Smith in the queue and thought that my ticket was for Gerald. In that case he would have seen the three of us talking together afterwards—which was why he had to grab my camera when he realized I'd taken a photo of him.

That was the last coherent thought I had for a long time. I slid into a nightmarish daze. I needed all my energy to fight the pain and the nausea. I didn't even have the strength to worry about what they had in store for us.

At some point I heard Finch say, "They're making an awful lot of noise."

I suppose we were both groaning.

"Close the window," Eddy said. "Put the radio on loud."

"Should we do something?" Julia suggested.

"Don't waste your pity. Compared to battery chickens they're in the lap of luxury."

I must have lost consciousness. I remember nothing more of that journey. The next thing I registered was the taste of a carpet.

Dust had collected between the fibres. When I opened my eyes I saw what looked like tiny grains of sand glinting at me. The carpet was grey. The light hurt my eyes, so I closed them.

All my senses were unnaturally sharp. There was a smell of food—of the tomato sauce you get in a can of baked beans and, more faintly, of something sweet yet acrid, like aftershave.

The carpet felt coarse and hard against my lips and my right cheek. I was lying on my stomach. The inside of my mouth was so dry it felt like sandpaper but there was no longer a gag in it. The pains in my body had subsided to a symphony of aches.

It was wonderfully quiet. My first thought was that they must have switched off the engine. Then I remembered that there wasn't a carpet in the camper. So they'd moved us.

I investigated my legs and arms. They weren't tied together. I couldn't find my right arm for a while. I grew quite panicky: maybe they'd chopped it off to send to Stephen Kinahan. Like sending Getty his grandson's ear, only more impressive. Eventually I discovered that I was lying on the arm, and my weight had made it completely numb. The arm might just as well have been dead. It didn't belong to me.

The next time I opened my eyes, I forced myself to keep them open. The light was harsh and electric: so it must be late evening or night-time. The carpet stretched away for what seemed like miles until it ended in a white wall. In the wall was a door. It was an ordinary hardwood door with rails, stiles and panels, not unlike our front door at home;

and it had a spyhole mounted in it. There was something odd about the door but I couldn't work out what.

I made a very big effort and moved my head so that it was resting on the other cheek.

Smith was lying beside me, her face turned away. For an instant I thought she was dead. Then I saw that she was breathing. I stretched out my left arm but she was too far away for me to reach.

"Smith," I whispered. "Smith."

She didn't answer. I tried to crawl towards her. My dead right arm let me down, literally. I collapsed. The movement had somehow restored the circulation. As the blood started moving, the agony was intense: it was all I could do to stop myself from shouting aloud. The pins and needles jabbed into my flesh.

Suddenly I realized what was odd about the door. It didn't have a door handle or even a keyhole. And the spyhole was facing into the room, not out of it.

I lacked the strength to explore our prison. Instead I lay still and tried to figure out what to do. Sooner or later someone would come to see us. The big question was whether or not I told them who I really was. Sooner or later, of course, they would find out—when they approached Stephen Kinahan with the ransom demand. But in the meantime there might be a temporary advantage for me to pretend to be Gerald. As far as PAF was concerned, Gerald Kinahan was a negotiable asset. Chris Dalham, on the other hand, was totally useless to them. Being Gerald might help keep me alive.

Smith stirred. She groaned.

Simultaneously I heard the sound of bolts being drawn back on the other side of the door.

"Still flat out," Finch said. He laughed in a determinedly jolly way, like Father Christmas trying to break the ice at a children's party.

"Get some water and splash it on their faces." The

second voice was male, thin and very precise: it made the hard consonants sound like a series of tiny explosions.

Smith groaned again.

"No need," said Finch. "It's wakey-wakey time."

"Who is that?" the stranger said. "The hair's all wrong. It's not young Kinahan."

"But you said – "

"Shut up!"

A hand grabbed my hair and yanked me up. I screeched with pain.

Smith rolled over. "You let him go," she shouted. "Who do you think you are?"

The man in the green shirt hauled me up. His face was about six inches away from mine. Eddy and Finch, both armed, were just behind him. The light gleamed on Eddy's white scalp. Julia hovered in the doorway. She looked almost as worried as I felt.

"Ah. The photographer." The man tugged my hair. "Who are you?"

"Chris Dalham. I'm a friend of Smith's."

He glanced at Smith. "Ms Weyburn's daughter. Pleased to meet you." He smiled at her for all the world as if this were an ordinary social occasion. "So where is Gerald Kinahan? At the concert?"

"He never meant to go to the concert," I said. "He's probably curled up at home with a good book. I just wish I could say the same for us."

Still smiling, the man gave me a back-handed blow across the cheek with his free hand.

"About five foot ten, you said," Eddy butted in. "Dark hair, blue eyes, at the concert with that girl—you can't blame us for getting the wrong bloke. Be reasonable, Heinrich."

"I am reasonable," the man with the green shirt said. He let go of my hair and straightened up. "I am always reasonable. If you want to blame anyone, other than yourself of course, you may blame this young man. If he hadn't interfered this morning you would have had a Polaroid of Gerald Kinahan."

The irony hit me: by taking a photo of Heinrich this morning I had indeed done Gerald a favour—but not the favour I had thought at the time. The net result was that I'd got kidnapped in Gerald's place.

Eddy hadn't finished. "If you'd done the job yourself, this wouldn't have happened."

"I told you," Heinrich said patiently. "After this morning the Garda would be looking for me in Dublin. I couldn't imperil the whole operation. Besides, I had other things to do. I thought I could rely on your intelligence."

"Are you saying–?"

"I'm saying that you made a mistake," Heinrich said. "Also, I am reminding you of the command structure of this operation. Thirdly, you would do well to remember that my detailed report on the operation will be seen by your superiors as well as mine."

Eddy showed his teeth and dropped his eyes.

"Ah well," Finch said, beaming through his beard at no one in particular. "We all make mistakes, eh?"

"As in Manchester?" Heinrich said coldly. "Perhaps PAF expects to make mistakes. We do things differently where I come from."

"I only meant – "

"I know what you mean." Heinrich paused. "Julia, you will have to delay the press release."

"Delay it?" she said. "Do you mean cancel it?"

He ignored her. "Where is Gerald?" he asked me.

"I don't know."

"Is he at the house on Bray Road South?"

"I told you, I don't know."

"Call them," Heinrich ordered Julia. "Ask to speak to Gerald—say you're a friend if they ask who you are. If he answers, or if they say they'll fetch him, just put the phone down."

Julia vanished.

Smith said, "May we have some water?"

"Later. When you've told me where Gerald is."

In a couple of minutes, Julia returned. "He's not there. A man answered—Stephen Kinahan, I think. He said Gerald was out."

Heinrich rubbed his chin. "Fetch me the little knife and the chopping board from the kitchen."

Julia's eyes widened. She opened her mouth.

"Go on," he said. "Quickly."

She obeyed.

"What are you going to do?" Smith said.

Heinrich smiled at her. "Hands are very delicate things. Very sensitive to pain."

Julia came back with a small single-edged knife and a square wooden chopping board.

"The trick is knowing where the nerves are," Heinrich went on. "I will give you a demonstration."

"What are you planning to do?" Smith said.

"Eddy and Julia will look after you, my dear." Heinrich gave her a little bow. "Our friend Finch is conveniently overweight: he will pin Chris to the floor. I myself will do the dissecting, of course—it's a skilled job. Oh—don't worry about the screaming. It doesn't matter. We don't mind. And there's no one else to hear."

He was so polite about it. So calm, so quiet. I stared at the grey carpet, at the dust and the glittering grains of sand. My head filled with a roaring noise that rose and fell like the surge of waves. I was listening to the sound of my own breathing. I was going to faint. I was glad.

"There's no need for all this," Smith said. She sat up and began to massage her ankles. "Gerald had a date with a girl—I don't know where, some winebar in central Dublin. But he was going to collect us after the concert. He said he'd wait for us in the bar opposite the Warehouse."

CHAPTER SIX

"Did you hear what Heinrich said?" Smith whispered. "Those guys did the Manchester bombing."

I nodded. We had huddled together to talk—partly for comfort and partly in case there was a microphone—in the middle of the grey carpet.

"But not Heinrich or Julia," I said. "And Heinrich's not part of PAF, or that's what it sounded like."

"Great. So who are they? The United Nations?"

"They're not bothering to wear masks. Did you notice that?"

Smith said nothing. I guessed from her face that she'd thought out the implications of that already. She glanced round the small, white room. Apart from the hardwood door with no handle, the only break in the monotony of the walls was a curtained window. We had checked that as soon as they'd left us alone. Behind the curtains was a steel plate screwed to the wall around the window embrasure. They'd even gone to the trouble of filing down the heads of the screws.

We'd need a crowbar to get out. We didn't have a crowbar. We didn't have anything—they'd emptied our pockets and even taken our watches before they put us in the room. There were the two of us, still weak after that hellish journey, against three men and a woman, at least two of whom were armed.

"Cooperation," Smith murmured. "It's our only chance. Make them think we're on their side. Maybe we'll get lucky."

I didn't believe it. Nor did she.

"Is your mother rich?" I said.

"Uh-huh."

"Maybe they don't know that. Maybe we should tell them."

"But what about you?"

I shrugged.

"If I go, we go," she said. "If you stay, I stay."

"Don't be stupid." I nuzzled her hair with my lips. "What do you think they're after?"

"Money, I guess."

"And publicity?"

I had this sudden vision of our vivisected corpses left lying by the side of the road. It made me shiver. Smith's arms tightened round my neck. The bolts on the far side of the door clicked back.

"How touching," Heinrich said. "It is like the fairy story, eh? You know it here? The infants abandoned in the forest."

"The babes in the wood," Finch said, scratching his beard.

Heinrich pointed at Smith. "Get up. You are coming with us."

"Where?"

"We are going to fetch Gerald Kinahan. You will help."

"Sure," Smith said. "Whatever you say. Look, I've got a lot of sympathy for – "

"Your friend stays here," Heinrich interrupted. "He will guarantee your good behaviour, eh? If you are foolish, he will pay for it. But you won't be foolish, will you?"

"Me? Of course not."

Heinrich clicked his fingers at Eddy and Finch, who came into the room.

"Just do as they say," he told me.

They pulled me away from Smith and made me lean against the wall with my feet together. Eddy poked my temple with the barrel of his gun. I jerked away from him. He poked even harder. Finch pulled my arms behind my back and bound my wrists and ankles with parcel tape.

He wound the tape over the cuffs of my shirt and jeans. I nearly said thank you. Last time they'd wrapped it round my bare skin.

"No gag this time?" Eddy said. He sounded disappointed.

"There's no need," Heinrich pointed out.

I was so grateful that I did say thank you.

They hustled Smith out of the room and shut the door behind them. I thought I might as well make myself as comfortable as possible. I hopped slowly to the nearest corner and managed to lower myself to the floor. With a lot more effort I got myself in a sitting position, with my back against the wall and my legs stretched out in front of me. All the time I listened. I heard nothing, not even the sound of an engine starting up.

It occurred to me that we couldn't be that far from Dublin—not if Heinrich planned to get back to the Warehouse before the concert ended and collect Gerald from the bar across the road. That cheered me up a little. With luck it meant that it wouldn't be long before Smith and I were together again. Then morale slumped even lower than before at the thought of having to share this little room with Gerald.

In a while the bolts shot back and Julia came in with an automatic in her hand. She was alone. For the first time I caught a glimpse of what was on the other side of the door: a little lobby, another doorway and, beyond that, a larger room. I saw the side of an armchair and the white door of a refrigerator.

Holding the gun well away from us both, she bent down and peered at my face. I wondered if she were short-sighted. Her features looked oddly out of focus: they lacked definition, as if whoever had made her had been in too much of a hurry to finish the job.

"Are you okay?" she said.

There were a number of possible answers to this, none of them polite. I changed the subject: "I could really use a drink of water."

She left the room, leaving the door ajar. I heard a tap running in a sink but no talking. A moment later she was back with a mug of water. Leaving the gun on the carpet, she crouched beside me and held the mug to my mouth.

Her hand was trembling and I was in a hurry: a lot of the water went on my shirt. She was so close to me I could have counted the freckles and blackheads on her face. She was still wearing the Warehouse tee-shirt. When I finished the water she collected the gun and fetched some more without my having to ask.

I gave her my best smile when she came back. "So they've all gone to Dublin, have they?"

She nodded.

"Are you part of the People for Animals Faction too?"

Instead of telling me to mind my own business she blushed as if I'd paid her a compliment and said, "Oh no, I'm just part of a supporters' group."

"You seem pretty active to me."

"Well, this is a one-off. They needed someone Irish, you see, someone with local knowledge."

In that case, I thought, they'd got themselves a turkey—if her knowledge of Irish geography was anything to go by. I drank half the water, more slowly this time. The gun was on the carpet. I had the feeling that Julia was almost as scared of it as I was. I lifted my head away from the mug. She shuffled away from me at once, as if afraid I might bite.

"You know something?" I said chattily. "I had no idea the Kinahans were mixed up with vivisection and stuff like that. It came as quite a shock, I can tell you. I'm a friend of Smith's, you see. I didn't even know the Kinahans existed until yesterday."

She still hadn't picked up the gun. "Are you on our side?" she said eagerly.

"Of course I am." I suppressed the memory of the meal that was at present being processed by my digestive system. "I've been a vegetarian for years. So's Smith."

"Everything we swallow," Julia said solemnly, "everything we wear, everything we touch: experimenting on animals has affected our whole lives. We live on a raft of animal suffering."

"I know. It's terrible." Thank God it was summer and I wasn't wearing my leather jacket. "What do you hope to get out of all this?"

For a moment she didn't answer and I feared she'd remembered who I was and why I was here. "What does it matter if I tell you?" she said. "Everyone will know when the press release goes out. We want money and publicity, of course. What else?"

I thought of the dead secretary in Manchester but decided it would be tactless to mention her.

"Stephen Kinahan and Astrid Weyburn are both guilty of crimes against animals," she went on. "The very worst sort of speciesism. So we're going to hold their children to ransom *and* whip up a lot of good publicity. They've both made their money by being cruel to animals, and we've got more right to it than they have. The publicity will force Kinahan to close Biercetown House. It'll make people realize just what the cosmetics industry does to animals."

"So—er—you're not planning to kill us?"

"Of course not," she said angrily. "What do you take me for? I wouldn't be here if there was any question of that. PAF's been into violence in the past, but all that's changed. Besides, Heinrich's organization is non-violent, and they're calling the shots because they're bankrolling the operation."

She was so worked up that I wondered if she were really trying to persuade herself, not me. Heinrich certainly hadn't struck me as the non-violent type, and if Finch and Eddy didn't want to give the wrong impression, they shouldn't go around waving guns in peoples' faces.

"I know this can't be very comfortable for you," she went on, her voice rising in volume, "but you can't make an omelette without breaking eggs, can you? And you have to look at your discomfort in context. I mean, think of it: three and half million animals a year are killed as a result of laboratory procedures. Tortured to death."

First Stephen Kinahan and now Julia wanted us to look at their arguments "in context". In both cases, "in context" seemed to mean that what they were doing was okay because someone else was doing something even worse.

"Would you like some more water?"

"No thanks."

"Are you sure now?"

I shook my head and started to hold my breath.

"If Kinahan and Weyburn are sensible, this won't last long," Julia said, looking at the carpet. "A week or two, maybe? Even just a few days—who knows?"

Still holding my breath, I screwed up my face. I'd last used this trick when I was about eleven. We used to have an RE teacher who fell for it every time.

"You won't tell the others I've been talking to you, will you?" she said. "They might—well, they might get the wrong idea. Heinrich's very strict about discipline and so on."

Was she never going to notice? I let out a groan.

"What's wrong?"

I shook my head from side to side. I groaned again.

"What is it?" As she bent over me her hair almost touched my face. "For God's sake what is it?"

"I—I need the toilet."

Apart from the freckles and blackheads her skin was so clear it seemed almost transparent. As she blushed, an ugly stain crept over her face. I bet she used to go to a convent school in the back of beyond, just like the RE teacher had done. I remembered to suck in my breath again.

"Look," she said, "I'm sorry but I can't – "

I keeled over to the floor and groaned once more.

"Oh Mother of God," she muttered.

I made my body twitch.

"I'll take you to the lavatory," she said suddenly. "But I'll be outside with the gun, all right? And don't bolt the door. No tricks, though. You promise?"

I nodded so violently my head banged against the wall.

Julia tried to pull me up. I made myself into a dead weight. She gave up. At last she realized that unless she actually came into the lavatory with me, she would have to free my hands, if not my ankles as well. She went out of the room and came back with a kitchen knife.

"I'll be covering you all the way, mind," she said. "And I'll tape you up again afterwards."

"Thank you," I gasped. "Quickly—I can't wait."

She slashed through the tape round my wrists. Moaning loudly, I wrapped my arms round her neck. This time I let her haul me up. We hobbled through the doorway into the little lobby. Beyond the lobby was a living-room-cum-kitchen. On the right was a flight of stairs and directly on our left was another door. She twisted the handle and pushed it open. Inside was a lavatory and basin. The window was so small that nothing much larger than a cat could have got through it.

"Get on with it," she said—almost harshly; I guessed she was regretting her kindness.

She ducked back into the room we'd come from. She wanted the gun—and also, perhaps, she was scared of seeing something the nuns might have advised her not to see. I made a retching noise to lull her suspicions and darted out of the lavatory.

Julia let out a screech. She flung herself at the gun. I grabbed the knob on one of the bolts and pulled the door towards me.

The door jarred against its frame. I rammed home the two bolts. They were new and shiny. There was also a lock with a key in it—and a blocked hole for the spindle of the handle that the door used to have. I turned the key and pocketed it.

She hammered on the door. I guessed she was using the butt of the automatic.

"Let me out," she screamed. "I'll shoot."

"Look," I said. "Be sensible. I really don't want you to get hurt."

"I mean it!"

"That looks like a hardwood door," I said, moving to the shelter of the wall. "You'll be lucky if you even make a hole in it, let alone shoot off two heavy bolts and a lock. And if you fire that gun the bullet could ricochet. You could kill yourself."

"You're just saying that."

"I am *not*," I yelled. "I'm trying to help you."

I meant it. One good turn deserved another. I'd only been able to fool her because—like the RE teacher—she was essentially a decent person. Even in these circumstances what I'd done made me feel a little guilty. Not much—but a little.

"I'm going to call the police," I said. "I'll make this as easy as I can for you. I don't think you realize what those men are capable of. They're going to kill us—can't you see? Otherwise they wouldn't have let us see their faces."

"I could kill you myself," she shrieked.

I hopped like a geriatric kangaroo into the living room. It was an impersonal place—no pictures on the walls, no TV, no books; some sort of holiday cottage, I guessed.

First a knife, then the phone. Julia was still banging on the door. I hopped into the kitchen area. The vegetable knife was on the other side of the locked door but I found a breadknife that did the job almost as well. I looked round for the phone. I knew there must be one, because Heinrich had sent Julia to phone the Kinahan house.

But the phone wasn't in the living room. I sidled into the lobby. The banging had stopped. Instead I heard a ragged tearing noise from the other side of the bolted door—it came regularly, as though someone were methodically

49

tearing up an old sheet for dusters. Suddenly I realized what it was: Julia was crying her heart out.

I felt awful about that. It's like my sister says: I'm too soft for the modern world.

I tiptoed upstairs. The first door led to a cramped bathroom. There were four sponge bags on the windowsill and four toothbrushes on the basin. I tried the other doors. Each led to a bedroom: one room had a Samsonite suitcase with a Lufthansa label round the handle; the second had a scuffed imitation-leather shoulder bag; and the third had two backpacks and far too much furniture in it—I guessed that the room downstairs had originally been a fourth bedroom. I couldn't find a phone.

As I toured the rooms I glanced out of all the windows. By now it was completely dark outside. When the lights were on, I just saw my own reflection in the glass. When I switched them off, I saw nothing at all.

I was in the middle of nowhere without a phone. And the only company I had was an armed female terrorist on the verge of a nervous breakdown.

CHAPTER SEVEN

I smelled the sea.

I remembered the sand on the grey carpet, and I shivered. Now the sun was down, it was cold. Since I'd last had an opportunity to notice the weather, a wind had sprung up and driven clouds across the sky. At least I assumed there were clouds up there. Either that or the stars were off-duty tonight.

I couldn't see the sea or hear it, but I could smell it. I glanced back at the house, a pale blur against the darkness. The light from the living-room window showed an area of hardstanding that divided the house from a high, ragged barrier that might have been a hedge.

What I really wanted to do was to run and shout and scream for help. But I didn't know where to run to, and there was no one to hear. Somewhere out in the darkness—probably driving towards me by now—were three lethal maniacs in a VW camper. And unless a miracle had happened, they still had Smith.

Panic swept over me in waves and I felt as though I were drowning. I made myself concentrate on something—on anything, it didn't matter what. If you're drowning, you're not picky about lifebelts.

If I was near the sea, the house must be north or south of Dublin. I tried to visualize a map of Ireland I'd seen on the ferry. County Dublin and County Meath were north of the capital and County Wicklow was south. In the van, Julia had mentioned that we had passed St Stephen's Green. So had the taxi—it seemed like years ago—on our way to the Warehouse. That must mean that this house, like Bray Road South, was somewhere south of Dublin. But not near Dublin itself: otherwise I would have heard the

51

sound of traffic and seen the yellow glow of a city smeared across the sky.

I put my money on County Wicklow. This was progress: "I'm somewhere in County Wicklow" made me feel a little less lost than "I'm somewhere in Ireland" had done.

My eyes gradually adjusted to the darkness as I walked round the house. I'd asked Julia where the phone was before I left. Her only reply was to tell me to commit an anatomical impossibility on myself. Then I'd asked her what they'd done with my watch and keys and money, and she ordered me to do something even more imaginative.

Julia had used a phone and she had only been gone for a moment or two. I hoped to find a public callbox on the doorstep. No such luck. If there wasn't a callbox she must have used a carphone. Beat-up VW campers don't usually have a carphone: therefore there must have been another vehicle, probably Heinrich's, on the premises.

Even if I could only find a car without a phone, I wouldn't have complained. I'm not choosy. With a bit of luck I could hot-wire it and get the hell out of here. I prayed for a car but my prayers weren't answered.

I staggered across an overgrown lawn, rounded another corner and walked into the hedge that bordered the hardstanding. A few yards further on I found the gate.

Outside was a road that ran past the house. The road, like the garden, sloped, which gave me the choice of going up or down. It was difficult to be sure in the near-darkness, but I reckoned it was shut in by hedges. I bent down and ran my hand over the surface. It was metalled but not covered with tarmac. Not a road that was likely to be going anywhere worth going to: just a track, really, designed for tractors not cars.

Up or down? Logically, I thought, going downhill would lead me towards the sea. Illogically, I didn't want to go there: with the sea at my back I would be trapped.

I began to walk up the lane. The lack of potential cover worried me: I had nowhere to hide from a car's headlights.

I broke into a run, stumbling over the ruts and skidding on loose stones. Gradually the slope of the lane became steeper. My heart thumped around in my chest like a wild thing trying to burst out of a cage. I don't know how long the lane was—a mile perhaps; it felt more like thirty. It's at times like this you discover how unfit you are.

The hedges dropped away. I burst into what seemed like an open space. I forced myself to stop and take bearings.

I'd reached a crossroads. The other three roads weren't much wider than the one I'd left, but at least they were surfaced with tarmac. No lights were visible but somewhere in the distance a dog was barking.

Between two of the roads a signpost leaned against the hedge. Or rather the post was there—but not the signs; some joker had ripped them off to confuse the invading armies of tourists.

There was nothing to choose between the three roads. I took the one on the right. In the unlikely event that my geographical calculations had come up with the correct answer, the right-hand road should run north—in the general direction of Dublin.

I had a stitch and my legs felt double their usual weight but I forced myself to start jogging. It wasn't just my own safety that worried me—though that was high on my list of priorities—it was Smith's. If Heinrich got back to the cottage and found me gone, he wasn't going to hang around and wait for the gardai. Either he would take Smith with him or he might decide to travel light—in which case her chances of staying alive would shrink to around vanishing point.

As I ran I listened. I knew that if I heard an engine I'd have to dive at the hedge and try to hide. Any vehicle on this road might belong to Heinrich, Eddy and Finch. What I needed was a telephone box or a house with a phone.

On the left-hand side of the road the hedge gave way to a wall. It was at least nine feet high, and it seemed higher because there was a belt of trees on the other side. I swore silently at it and crossed the road so I was running beside the hedge on the opposite side. The wall cut by fifty per cent my chances of seeing lights in the distance or, in an emergency, finding cover.

I jogged on, hoping that I would be able to hear the sound of an approaching car above the racket I was making: the pounding of my heart, my gasps for breath and the bone-jarring slaps of my trainers on the tarmac.

Then I saw light.

It was so faint at first that I couldn't be sure. Just a glimmering along the top of the wall, most of it blocked by the leaves on the trees. I ran on, trying not to get excited.

Gradually the light increased in strength. It was never exactly bright but a gap in the trees gave me a better view of the wall: a triple line of barbed wire ran along the top, set at an angle so it overhung the road.

The wall swung away from the road. I followed. The light was stronger here—but still no more than a faint golden glow, a fringe that separated the top of the wall from great darkness of the sky above.

Gravel crunched beneath my feet. I slowed to a halt. I was standing in a three-sided enclosure like an equilateral triangle, with the road as the baseline and the wall running the other sides. At the apex of the triangle, the point furthest from the road, were a couple of flat-roofed buildings with what looked like a pair of gates strung between them.

I gasped with relief and walked up to the gates. They were closed and pretty solid—two sheets of steel nearly twice my height, and topped with more barbed wire. Not exactly inviting, I thought, but there were lights on the other side, and that meant people and probably a phone.

I looked round for a bell or something but in the semi-darkness I couldn't find a polite way of announcing myself. So I banged on the gates with the palms of my hands.

"Hey!" I shouted. "Anybody home?"

At once a couple of dogs began to bark. At first they sounded quite a long way off but the barks drew rapidly nearer. It wasn't a comfortable feeling. I felt as though they were hunting me down.

Still barking, the dogs slammed into the gates. There they were, maybe a couple of inches away from me, slavering for my blood.

I cleared my throat and tried diplomacy: "Good doggies," I said. "Where's your master?"

That made them bark even louder. Where were their owners? It couldn't be that late but maybe people went to sleep early in the country.

I banged on the gates again to give myself something to do. The dogs were making so much noise I might as well have saved my strength. They went on barking for another minute.

The lights went on. The shock of it was intense—as though someone had actually hit me. The brightness hurt. I covered my eyes with my hands. The forecourt couldn't have been much brighter under a noonday sun. There were two lights, I think, each mounted on one of the buildings at either side of the gates.

"You are being recorded by video camera," a voice boomed out from the sky. "A copy of the tape will be sent to the Garda."

"Look," I yelled, "that's fine—I want to phone the Garda myself. I – "

"You are advised that any attempt to enter these premises will be at your own risk," the voice went on; it sounded cracked and distorted, as if the loudspeaker were finding it hard to cope. "No access to unauthorized personnel."

"Will you just listen to me for a moment?"

"All trespassers will be prosecuted," the voice intoned. "These premises are protected by armed security guards and dogs."

"Could you at least tell me where I can find a phone?"

55

"You are being recorded by video camera . . . A copy of the tape will be sent to the Garda . . . "

A recorded message by a gunslinging bureaucrat? I couldn't even be sure there was a person on the other side of the gates. Besides, the dogs were barking so loudly there was no chance of making myself heard. It needled me so much that I gave the video camera a couple of one-fingered salutes to record for posterity.

I backed out of the forecourt. The lights stayed on and the dogs didn't let up either. What was the place, anyway? Some sort of government installation? It didn't have a sign outside it, not even BEWARE OF THE DOG.

The disappointment drained the energy out of me. For what seemed like hours I'd been running on adrenalin, and suddenly the tank was empty.

On my left the wall looked like going on for ever. I staggered a few yards along the road. A farm track went off to the right. Unlike the road itself it had grassy verges. I turned in and sat down to have a rest. If I were lucky the security guards would come out to move me on. Even security guards are human beings. If I could just talk to them face to face, maybe I could persuade them to phone the cops for me. I decided that in a moment I would go and squat on the gravel and howl at the dogs until somebody came.

The grass was damp with dew and not exactly level, but to me it felt like an interior-sprung mattress. I was tempted to lie down. I knew I mustn't do that. My anxiety for Smith had turned into a dull but savage ache and settled somewhere in the region of my stomach.

I heard the sound of an engine. I struggled to my feet and moved a few yards down the track. The lights on the forecourt were still on so I had a good view of what happened.

An orange van flashed by: the VW camper on its way back to the house. I was too late. In a few minutes they'd find I'd gone, and then God alone knew what would happen to Smith. I moved to the head of the lane. I had to try those gates again: it was my only chance.

But there was another engine approaching. I was about to leap into the road and start waving my arms about when I remembered that Heinrich and his friends must have taken two vehicles.

The second one sounded like a car, and it was slowing down. My morale surged upwards out of the depths. A car stopping here couldn't have anything to do with Heinrich.

I'd left it too late. The car had passed the mouth of the track before I had time to reach the road. Its brake lights glowed.

The car pulled into the forecourt in front of the gates. It was one of those big Nissan saloons—dark-blue, with Irish plates.

The dogs, who had been showing signs of quietening down, went off their rockers once again. I was just about to cross the road when one of the car's nearside doors opened. The light gleamed on a bald scalp.

It was Eddy.

I shrank back into the patch of shadow at the mouth of the track. Eddy opened another car door. Gerald Kinahan got out.

He'd changed since I'd last seen him—smartened himself up for giving the girlfriend the push. He had his hair slicked back and he was wearing the sort of jacket that doesn't leave you much change from a couple of hundred quid.

"You are being recorded by video camera . . . A copy of the tape will be sent to the Garda . . . "

Gerald sauntered up to the gates with Eddy close beside him. I saw them looking at a small dark rectangle set in one of the gateposts. Some sort of intercom? A keypad for an electronic lock?

A moment later the dogs stopped barking. It was as though they'd been switched off at the mains. The silence was deafening. Gerald and Eddy waited, their heads bowed.

Slowly, very slowly, the gates swung backwards on their hinges.

CHAPTER EIGHT

I ran straight across the road. For a few long seconds, a few long yards, I was in full sight of anyone on the gravel. I was banking on their attention being on the gates.

No one shouted. No one's feet crunched towards me on the gravel. I crept along the line of the wall until I reached the angle where it began to turn in towards the gates.

I crouched down and moved noiselessly on to my hands and knees. My head was no more than a foot above the ground. I inched forward and peeped round the corner.

Try as I might I couldn't get a good view of the interior of the Nissan. Someone was in the driver's seat. There might also be someone in the back but I wasn't sure. In any case, Smith could be out of sight—in the well between the seats, for example, or stuffed in the boot. Alternatively she could be in the camper.

The gates were fully open. Beyond them stretched an avenue lined with trees. A grey-haired man in a blue uniform came out of a doorway in the lodge on the left.

"Sorry to knock you up so late, McGowan," Gerald said. "Bit of a flap on about some figures."

He sounded almost normal—in other words, superior, smarmy and so self-confident he was an offence to the eardrums. But he spoke more loudly than usual—maybe McGowan was deaf or maybe Gerald was nervous.

McGowan had a holster on his belt and a frown on his face. He looked at Eddy. "It's a wee bit irregular, Mr Kinahan. I'll have to issue temporary ID for this gentleman."

"Ah yes—this is Doctor O'Brien from UCD," Gerald said. "By the way, why are the lights on?"

"We had a bit of bother just before you arrived—one of

the boyos from the village had a drop too much, I think. You know what they're like on Saturday night. Nothing we couldn't handle."

"Who else is on tonight?"

"Just Reardon. He's monitoring the TV screens in case our boyo hasn't given up."

"Get him out here, will you? I want a word with you both."

"What about?"

"I've got a message from my father, and I don't want to have to say it twice. He's thought of a contingency we didn't cover in the security review. It's urgent."

McGowan shrugged. His body language made it clear that he didn't like being ordered about by someone young enough to be his son. He put his head in the doorway. "Michael," he shouted. "Come on out a moment."

The driver's door of the Nissan swung silently open. Heinrich slid out. He was carrying a gun. I knew who it was despite the khaki Balaclava helmet that covered his head. I recognized the plump haunches and the narrow shoulders, the green shirt and the baggy white trousers.

He skipped into the gateway. As I had learned to my cost in Dublin, he was surprisingly agile for someone with such an ungainly figure. Simultaneously, Reardon came through the doorway. He saw Heinrich prancing towards him, and his hands dived to the holster on his belt.

McGowan spun round. "What the–?"

Gerald took a step backwards. If his body was talking, it was saying, "Leave me out of this, please."

"Hands on heads," Heinrich snapped.

Reardon fumbled at the buckle of his holster. He was younger than McGowan, and he was panicking.

"No, Michael!" McGowan yelled.

And Heinrich fired.

Seeing the effect of a bullet at first hand is a horrible. I suppose we've all been conned by TV cop shows and movies. In reality there are no nice, clean bullet wounds, and the victims don't collapse gracefully on the ground. It's messy, it's painful, and it makes you feel that life would be a whole lot better if dolphins and whales had the running of planet earth.

The bullet caught Reardon in the left shoulder. Its impact knocked him against the open door. He bounced off and, turning as he fell, landed face down across the threshold. Even at a distance, the bullet's exit wound on his back wasn't look a pretty sight.

And the soundtrack made it worse: the noise Reardon made, which was halfway between a scream and a gasp, and the thud of his falling body, a deadweight like a sack of potatoes hitting the ground. The crack of the shot set the dogs barking again. They must have been shut in the lodge in case they savaged the boss's son.

Gerald Kinahan slumped against the gatepost and was sick. That made me dislike him a little less.

"Get their guns," Heinrich said.

By now McGowan had his hands on his head. His whole body was trembling, and so for that matter was mine. Eddy sidled up to him and relieved him of his automatic.

"And the other guy's," Heinrich said, raising his voice to be heard above the barking.

Eddy obeyed.

"I want the car in the drive," Heinrich went on. "And *you*"—he pointed his gun at McGowan—"are going to quieten those damned animals and shut the gates behind us. Oh, and I want the lights out."

He herded McGowan past Reardon's body and into the building.

Eddy grinned at Gerald. "You're driving, squire. I'll ride shotgun and mind the baby."

While all this was going on—and it only took a few seconds—my brain was burning rubber trying to work out what to do. Where was Smith? It looked as if I'd misread what Heinrich intended: this wasn't just a kidnap operation. I wasn't the only one who'd got it wrong—Julia had, as well.

This place was Biercetown House, the Kinahans' research laboratory. Heinrich was using Gerald as his passport to get inside. Maybe that was what he'd planned all along.

Whether Smith was at the house or in the car, I still needed to get to a phone. The nearest phone was here, at Biercetown House. So I had a choice: either I wandered around the Irish countryside, hoping to find a telephone box—or I headed for the nearest phone and took a chance on whether or not I'd be able to use it.

There were two more shots in quick succession—muffled by the walls of the building. Gerald put his hands over his face. I guessed that Heinrich was quietening the dogs by the simplest way he knew. For an animal activist, shooting dogs seemed a little inconsistent; but maybe guard dogs counted as honorary humans in Heinrich's scale of values.

Eddy and Gerald got in the car.

The overhead lights went out. The Nissan's engine fired and its headlights came on full-beam, creating a brilliantly-lit tunnel through the gates and up the drive. By contrast, everywhere else seemed very dark.

The Nissan moved slowly forwards. Gerald was revving the unfamiliar engine too high.

I'll ride shotgun and mind the baby. Smith had to be somewhere inside the Nissan.

My legs made the connection and made the decision before my mind did. I scrambled up. Bending low, I sprinted across the gravel. Heinrich and McGowan were still inside the lodge on the left. Gerald was concentrating on driving and Eddy was concentrating on Gerald. The Nissan covered the sound of my movements, and I reckoned that if I kept in the shadows I had a good chance of staying out of sight.

I was no more than a couple of yards behind the car as it went through the gateway. I slipped round to the off-side as we went in—away from Eddy, away from the lighted doorway of the building on the other side of the drive. The matching building on my side of the gateway was in darkness.

The car stopped. There was a *whirring* behind me. The gates were moving. Slowly and almost silently they swung closed. The automatic locks engaged with a series of clicks.

I crouched below the level of the car's windows and edged between it and the wall of the darkened building. I heard Gerald whimpering through the open window. By the Nissan's front off-side wheel, the wall made a right-angled turn into a patch of deeper shadow. I followed it and walked straight into a clump of nettles.

The next few minutes were agony. Both my hands had been stung. I tucked them into my armpits and squeezed, hoping to dull the pain. At the same time I had to find out what was going on.

"Get out," Eddy said to Gerald.

Two car doors slammed.

I heard Eddy say, "What have you done with the other bloke?"

"He's neutralized," Heinrich said. "Nothing to worry about—both of them will live. Now, who else is here?"

"Just the nightshift technicians I told you about," Gerald said, stumbling over the words in his eagerness to be helpful. "There's only the two of them. They'll be up at the lab, I imagine."

"You're sure?"

"I *promise*," Gerald wailed.

"Any chance they'll come down to see what all the noise is about?"

"I—I doubt it. The dogs are always barking, especially on Saturday nights."

"What if they heard the shots?"

"They'll ignore them. There's sometimes shooting on the farms round here at night. Your only problem will be the phone-check."

"Explain."

"But I told you in the car."

"Tell me again."

Gerald could hardly wait. "Well, it's our new system, you see. During the night the security people have to call the Garda headquarters in Phoenix Park at two-hourly intervals. I think they must have made the last call about ten minutes ago."

"You *think*? Last time you were certain. If you're lying . . . "

"No, I'm sure. Ask McGowan, he'll – "

Gerald broke off, as if he'd suddenly realized that McGowan might not be in a position to answer questions right now. There was a long pause in the conversation. I was longing for them to get up the drive and leave me free to look for a phone. If they left McGowan down here, and if he were more or less undamaged, he might make a useful ally.

Then Heinrich said, "So if you're right, we've got almost two hours to play with. Where's the switchboard?"

"Here in the lodge," Gerald said. "The control room with the closed-circuit TV monitors is on your left, and the switchboard's on your right. As you go in, I mean. It's – "

"Do all lines go through the switchboard?" Heinrich interrupted.

"Yes. Even my father hasn't got a private line."

Heinrich's next words made me realize that I'd miscalculated. All I'd done was walk of my own accord into a trap. My pathetic little plan of phoning the Garda hadn't a hope in hell of succeeding.

"Right," he said, and by his change of tone I guessed that he was talking to Eddy: "I'll look after Mister Kinahan. I want you to stay on the gate until Finch comes back. Then you let them in and come to join me in the lab. And in the meantime you can make yourself useful. There's no point in taking chances. So get the axe out of the boot and sort out the video and the switchboard."

CHAPTER NINE

Mind the baby?

As the Nissan rolled slowly up the avenue of trees, I leaned against the stone wall at the back of the lodge. I watched the car's tail-lights flickering along the tree trunks. I tried to stop my teeth chattering. I tried to do some positive thinking about my negative image of myself. I felt like a humanoid jelly—quivering with fear and indecision. Well, so what? Any normal person would have felt the same.

In the other lodge across the drive, Eddy was going bananas with the axe. As he swung it down he yowled like a berserk Viking. Next I'd hear sounds of cracking and splintering as the blade smacked into its target. Then there'd be a happy grunt as Eddy pulled the axe back for the next blow. He was enjoying his work.

I had to face it: I was in a worse position than I had been ten minutes before. The wall and the gates could keep people in as well as keep them out. Communications with the outside world were in the process of being phased out. One security guard was wounded, and I was afraid that the other might be in the same condition. I didn't feel very optimistic about the two nightshift technicians up at the lab. As for Gerald, he was totally absorbed in trying to save his own greasy skin. I couldn't altogether blame him.

So I was on my own with just a couple of terrorists to cope with. Or rather four terrorists, because Finch and Julia would soon be turning up with the news that I'd done a runner.

Eddy yowled. *Crunch* went the axe. Eddy grunted.

The only silver lining to this particular cloud was that

the last place they'd expect to find me was at Biercetown House. They had me in a trap but they didn't know it. I knew what any sane person in my position would do. A place like this must have huge grounds—the drive seemed to go on for ever, and there was no sign of a house at the end of it. A sane person would make himself inconspicuous and twiddle his thumbs. Sooner or later the gardai would arrive, alerted by the security guards' failure to make their two-hourly phone call. A sane person would then weasel out of the undergrowth and receive a police commendation for his courage and common sense.

The trouble is, as I've been forced to realize on other occasions, where Smith is concerned I'm not entirely sane.

Mind the baby?

That had made it sound as if she were in the car. But if she were, I didn't think she could be able to talk. She's not the sort of person who allows people to walk all over her. I'd have heard her cursing them through the windows of the car. When Eddy opened the boot—if she'd been inside and had the use of her arms and legs—she'd have gone for him with the axe.

I thought about the alternative—if Smith wasn't in the Nissan she'd be in the VW camper. There was in fact a third option: that Smith had served her purpose so they'd put a bullet in her head and dumped her in a ditch or at the house. I couldn't face thinking about that.

So: either Smith was already here at Biercetown House or she'd soon be arriving with Finch and Julia in the VW. All I had to do was find her, rescue her and take her somewhere safe to wait for the Garda. Simple—any fool could do it.

Eddy yowled. *Crunch* went the axe. Eddy grunted.

I don't want to give the wrong impression. All this makes it seem as if I were cool-headed and clear-thinking and just bursting to do something heroic. Well I wasn't. I was shaking with fear. Thanks to the nettles, my hands felt as though they were on fire. If my self-pity could have been turned into water, it would have drowned the entire population of Ireland and left some over for Wales.

Why me? I kept thinking. *Why does it have to be me?*

In the end I left the shelter of the nettles and slipped into the long avenue of trees. This was not the result of a rational decision. It was just that doing something was better than doing nothing, and that listening to Eddy's axework was making my skin crawl. It seemed all too likely that once he'd finished on the switchboard he would shoulder the axe and stroll round looking for something else to chop up.

Also—*Mind the baby* . . . The Nissan was a better bet than the VW. And the Nissan should have a phone.

At first I moved slowly, taking care to make as little noise as possible. The drive was long and straight and covered with gravel. On either side was a row of old trees—don't ask me what sort: these had the regulation green leaves, and the twisting branches of each tree had tangled with those of its neighbours. The avenue was flanked by small fields dotted with clumps of smaller trees. The reason I knew all this was that there were lights at strategic points along the avenue and along the wire fences that defined the fields. The place wasn't floodlit—there were huge areas of shadow between the lights. But the lighting was more than enough to make the average intruder feel nervous.

I knew there might be electronic boobytraps as well, but there was nothing I could do about them except hope that Eddy in his enthusiasm had destroyed anything that looked vaguely electrical.

I avoided the gravel and ran along the strip of grass on the right. I scuttled from tree to tree, from shadow to shadow. The sound of the axework diminished in volume as I moved further from the gates. Every now and then I looked back: the light from the lodge grew smaller and smaller, and finally it vanished altogether. By now

I was running, knowing that Eddy could no longer hear or see me.

A lot of rabbits were frolicking around, their tails gleaming when they lolloped through one of the circles of light. Obviously no one had told them what was being done to their cousins up in the research laboratory. They all ran away from me, which was good for morale: it made me feel formidable and dangerous. Even rabbits have their uses.

The drive went on and on. I was running uphill—not much of a gradient, but enough to make things difficult. The sweat streamed down my face and back. As I ran I was straining to hear the sound of an engine—the Nissan in front of me or the VW behind. If either of them came along, I'd be uncomfortably exposed to their headlights.

There was still no sign of the research laboratory. I was beginning to wonder if I'd made a mistake. The grounds were even larger than I'd thought. I'd already covered at least half a mile. The folks at Biercetown House liked their privacy. I could spend the rest of the night jogging between their gates and their front door.

The drive levelled out and widened. The wind strengthened. Without warning the trees stopped and the grass verge gave way to gravel. On the left, fields speckled with lights stretched downhill as far as the eye could reach. On the right, set back a few yards from the line of the drive, was a great, grey ghost of a house.

I think the dim lighting must have made it seem larger than it was. Six pillars soared up the front to the roof. In the middle was a double flight of steps leading to a front door that looked big enough to take a Transit van with a roof rack. Two rows of windows stretched across the facade. The sills of the lower row were several feet above my head, which gives you an idea of the building's scale.

Lights glowed faintly in all the windows. I was going mad. Tall green giants, their swaying bodies twisted into impossible shapes, were pressing against the glass and peering out at me.

My hair lifted on my head. I took a step back, ready for flight. Then the truth hit me. These weren't giants but trees growing *inside* the house. Their branches were moving in the breeze. The whole place was just a shell filled with assorted vegetation that was blindly groping towards the windows and trying to reach the light.

The house was a ruin. Now I could see that only a few of the windows still had their glass. The lights that gave the place the illusion of being inhabited were just the usual security lamps.

I walked quickly along the frontage of the house, careless of the noise my feet made on the loose stones. I don't mind admitting the place spooked me. There was a painted sign leaning against the steps to the front door: DANGER. FALLING MASONRY.

The house ended in a long wall pierced by an archway. Just inside was a red-and-white boom in the "up" position. Another sign had been fixed to the wall. BIERCETOWN HOUSE SCIENTIFIC ESTABLISHMENT. ALL VISITORS MUST REPORT TO RECEPTION.

This visitor had other ideas. I sidled through the archway and ducked immediately to my right. I took cover behind one of two big cylindrical dustbins on wheels.

Everything was quiet and still. I was in a brightly-lit yard that had originally been designed for horses. On my right was the wall of the house, towering like a stone cliff and streaked around the doorways and window openings with the blackened evidence of fire. In front of it was a low rope barrier with another notice saying DANGER. FALLING MASONRY.

On my left was a two-storey range which must have escaped when the main house was gutted. Now it had been refurbished with a lot of plate glass and fresh paint and prettified with hanging baskets and tubs of flowers. There were signs all over the place—to reception, the staff restaurant, the computer complex and so on. None of them mentioned the animal house. Maybe everyone knew where that was.

On the fourth side, facing the archway, was a modern building that ran the whole width of the yard. It looked like a cross between a purpose-built light-industrial unit and a small office block. There were lights in several of the uncurtained windows but I could see no one inside. Three cars were parked in front of this building. I assumed that two of them belonged to the technicians. The third was Heinrich's Nissan.

Mind the baby?

I ran as softly as I could across the yard to the car. The VW might arrive at any moment—and with it the news that I had escaped; I didn't have time to be subtle. Running across the yard sounds riskier than in fact it was: I guessed that whatever Heinrich and Gerald were doing, they wouldn't have much time for gazing out of the window.

The car was unlocked and it had a phone. I wondered if I could make it work, and if 999 was the emergency number in Ireland. The key was still in the ignition. I threw a glance behind the front seats—Smith wasn't there—and fumbled around for the catch that operated the boot.

I ran to the back of the car. The boot was empty. Disappointment twisted through me like a knife. Either Heinrich had taken Smith into the building or she was with Finch and the VW.

As I shut the boot, so gently that it made barely a sound, I caught sight of a familiar shape on the parcel shelf behind the back seat. It was my camera. I opened the near-side back door and stretched my arm along the shelf. My fingers closed round the Zeiss Ikon.

At that very moment I heard the rising note of an engine on the drive. The brakes squealed. The engine note faltered and then rose as the driver changed down for the tight right-hand turn into the archway.

A dog began to bark. It wasn't that far away. One by one, other dogs joined in.

I scrambled into the Nissan and shut the door behind me. A black Land Rover nosed into the yard. Now who the hell was this? It drove slowly towards me. Before I ducked down I glimpsed another vehicle edging through the archway: here, at last, was the orange VW camper.

CHAPTER TEN

"Time's running out," Heinrich said. "I want to leave in ten minutes maximum. We'll use the other gates."

He'd come out of the building with a briefcase in his hand and Gerald at his heels. They'd passed right beside the Nissan without even glancing through the partly-open windows. Gerald now had his hands taped behind his back. Heinrich was still wearing his Balaclava.

"Before we go," Heinrich said, "we need to – "

Finch stuck his head out of the VW's window. "We got a problem. That kid's escaped from the cottage. He locked Julia in."

Eddy had climbed out of the black Land Rover. It was unmarked but I guessed it belonged to the security guards. I rolled down the Nissan's rear offside window a little further. Trying the phone would have to wait. Eddy had an automatic poking out of the pocket of his combat jacket and the axe over his shoulder. You could tell by the way he moved—all strut and bounce and swagger—that he really fancied himself as the height of terrorist chic.

Julia jumped down from the passenger side of the VW and ran over to Heinrich. Finch followed more slowly, scratching his beard and looking mildly depressed. The harsh overhead lights stripped the colours out of everything. The yard looked like a B movie set for a concentration camp.

"What about the animals?" Julia said. "Have you let them out? Why didn't you tell me you were coming to Biercetown House?"

"Jesus, woman," Eddy said. "That was the whole point of the operation right from the start. Why do you think we went back for young Kinahan?"

Heinrich ignored the interruption. "You little fool," he said to Julia, which I thought was surprisingly restrained in the circumstances. "How did he do it?"

"He tricked me," she wailed. "Made out he was ill and needed to use the toilet."

"When was this?"

"I—I don't know exactly. It wasn't long after you went."

"But that was hours ago," Eddy said. "I'm surprised the cops aren't here already."

"It's a good sign," Heinrich said. "Use your head: it means he probably went downhill from the cottage—towards the sea. If he did, he won't meet a soul till dawn."

"We've got to get out of here," Eddy said.

"Not yet,' Heinrich said calmly. "More haste, less speed, eh? Anyway, the boy doesn't know we're here—that's the main thing. No one does. So there's no need to panic."

"But what about the animals?" Julia said. "Now we're here, we've got to free them. We can't just – "

"Shut up, you stupid cow." Eddy hefted the axe on to his other shoulder. "All you do is cause problems."

Finch flapped his arms at both of them. "Calm down, will you?" He turned to Heinrich. "More to the point, what about our baby?"

"Baby?" Julia screeched. "Whose baby?"

"This baby's a bomb," Eddy said. "Can't you stop asking these boneheaded questions?"

"What bomb?" Julia said.

"That's what the briefcase is for, love," Finch explained. "Now don't fret. We know what we're doing."

"No problems there," Heinrich said. "I can sort it out in a couple of minutes."

Eddy jumped as if someone had wired him to a power-point. "You mean you haven't done it yet? What have you been doing, for God's sake?"

"You just don't learn, do you?" Heinrich said in a flat, cold voice like a slap in the face. "If nothing else, you'd have thought that foul-up at Manchester would have taught you the value of a preliminary survey. Time spent on reconnaissance is never wasted. I've also had to deal with those two technicians."

Eddy shrivelled. He looked at Finch for moral support.

Finch said, "Where will you put the baby?"

It was weird, I thought, how they didn't like calling a bomb a bomb. But where was Smith?

"The director's office." Heinrich gestured at the block behind the line of cars. "It's nice and central. It's between this building and the animal house."

"The animal house!" Julia yelped, distracted from the baby. "We've got to get the animals out."

"You can go right in," Heinrich said. "Everything's unlocked now. My friend Gerald has kindly disabled the electronic central-locking system. It controls every lock in the complex. All in all, in fact, Gerald has been *very* helpful."

Gerald looked at his feet.

"You see," Finch said soothingly to Julia. "Plenty of time for the animals. All being well, that is."

"But no one's going to get killed, are they?" Julia asked; her voice was getting higher and higher. "We never discussed that. I won't let you, do you hear?"

I'd opened the camera without knowing what I was doing. It still had a roll of film in it. I thought, *Why not?* While they were talking, I set the aperture, exposure length and focus.

As I've said, the yard was brightly-lit but even so I didn't rate my chances highly, not without flash. I cocked the camera. Still, I thought, Zeiss Ikons are remarkable machines and in photography there's always an element of luck. I knelt on the back seat, rested the camera on the parcel ledge, framed the shot and pressed the shutter.

73

Heinrich ignored Julia completely. "Get the girl out now," he said. "You'd better free her legs."

Finch slid back the side door of the camper and helped Smith into the yard. He cut the tape round her ankles but left her wrists tied behind her back. She wasn't gagged. They looked at her while she rubbed some life back into her ankles. Then she straightened up.

"You're a bunch of ratbags," she said conversationally, raking her eyes round the five of them.

I folded up the camera and, out of habit, slipped my hand through the carrying strap. I scrambled between the front seats and wriggled behind the wheel. Now was the time to try the phone. I could still see and hear what was happening.

"Go and stand over there," Heinrich said. He pointed at the smoke-blackened wall of the main house. "Between that window and the doorway. You too, Gerald. I want you both to face the wall. It'll be safer for you."

I picked up the handset and punched in 999. Nothing happened. Gerald took a few uncertain steps towards the wall. He stopped and glanced at the empty doorways and the rows of blank windows. This side of the house wasn't as grand as the front. It was like a derelict prison. Gerald looked over his shoulder at Smith, who hadn't moved.

"Why?" she said to Heinrich.

"Just do as I say. It's for your own good, I assure you. You won't get hurt."

Smith's chin lifted. "You going to shoot us or something?"

"No, of course not," Julia said. "We're civilized people here."

"Dear God," Smith said. "Is this what you call civilized? I'm not going anywhere."

"Don't be foolish," Heinrich yelled at her.

"Then why?"

As Smith spoke, I knew I had to do something. I fiddled with the switches on the phone. The LED remained unlit.

The damn thing wouldn't even bleep at me. There just wasn't time to experiment. I didn't have the ghost of a plan. I didn't have a weapon. I looked desperately round the car. Suddenly I realized that I did have a weapon of a sort. I was sitting in it.

"No one's going to get killed," Julia said. She started by making a statement and ended by asking a question.

Eddy wrapped his arm round her neck and squeezed.

"Look, I really don't see why I should make it easy for you," Smith said. "Do you?"

The camera, swinging loose on my wrist, banged against the gearstick. The car had an automatic shift like my dad's. R for reverse. Easy, I told myself in an effort to boost confidence. Like taking candy from a baby.

The trouble was, my experience of driving was limited. I know plenty of theory but I haven't had much practice. My sister's boyfriend is a mechanic. He's taken me out a few times in his Capri—without licence, insurance, road tax or L-plates: highly illegal. Still, they say that the best way of learning anything is the hands-on method. Learn as you go. Just in time, I remembered to release the handbrake.

"They're going to let us go, Smith," Gerald said loudly. "They promised. If I cooperated, they said they'd – "

"Go tell it to the fairies," Smith said. "We've seen their faces, heard their voices."

I twisted the key in the ignition. The engine fired and I yanked the stick from park to reverse. The car rolled backwards. I hung on to the steering wheel and rammed the accelerator into the floor.

The revs hit the red. The Nissan bucked. The tyres fought to get a grip on the gravel. For an instant I smelled the stench of burning rubber. Then we were off.

I backed in a wide, wavering arc. I tried with only partial success to look where I was going. There were too many distractions. Six people were in the way, and they all jumped for their lives.

Things got even more confused. Heinrich started yelling. Eddy let go of Julia and threw the axe at the car. It landed on the roof and bounced off. Gerald and Smith broke into a run, but not in the same direction.

I lost control of the steering wheel. The Nissan crashed through the rope barrier, ran over the DANGER notice and ended up at the wall of the main house. I braked too late. The rear of the car smacked into the wall with a jolt that jarred my whole body.

Gerald ran through the archway and disappeared into the night. Smith sprinted towards me, her hands still tied behind her back. I leant across to open the passenger door. It was just as well.

One moment the windscreen was as good as new. The next time I looked, it had turned into an opaque mosaic of fragments. There was a neat round hole above the steering wheel.

I wriggled through the nearside door, and collapsed in a heap at Smith's feet. I grabbed her arm and hauled myself up. Her face was dead white, apart from a fresh bruise on her left cheekbone.

"Chris," she said. And she tried to smile.

The car was between us and whoever was shooting. Another bullet smacked into the bonnet. The VW's engine fired. Someone with his wits about him—I think it must have been Finch—backed the camper into the archway and stopped. We were trapped in the yard.

"Come on out," Heinrich yelled.

He and Eddy had taken cover behind the wing of the Land Rover. Only Julia was still in the open. She was running towards the technicians' cars.

"You can't escape," Heinrich went on. "If you have a weapon, throw it down where we can see it and come out with your hands in the air. With the girl. Otherwise I put a bullet in the fuel tank."

I wondered if he knew who had been behind the wheel of the car.

"You want to fry?" Heinrich said. "I'll count to five."

"Move," Smith said.

"But where?" Even as I spoke, she seemed to vanish under the car. My attention had been on the yard, not the wall behind me. Now I realized that I'd rammed the car into the top of a basement doorway that was two-thirds below the level of the yard. The Nissan's rear nearside wheel was actually in mid-air over the stone steps that ran down to the basement.

I followed Smith—not exactly gracefully: in fact I fell down the steps and ended up in a heap across the threshold.

"Move," she yelled again. Head down, she was struggling like an armless maniac through what looked like a small forest of brambles and nettles and tree trunks.

Someone in the yard loosed off two shots. One of them smacked into stonework and whined off at an angle; I don't know where the other one went. I crawled after Smith. I could barely see. My eyes were still dazzled by the lights outside. A thorn slashed my cheek.

There was a third shot, followed by a couple of seconds of silence. Time became elastic and stretched all the way to infinity. The camera had snagged on a fallen branch. I struggled to free my wrist from the strap. The worn leather snapped.

Then came a massive *whumph*. A cushion of air rushed down the steps: a blow like a slap from a giant's hand threw me flat on my face.

Everything was very bright and very hot. I closed my eyes.

CHAPTER ELEVEN

The further we burrowed, the darker it became.

I felt like the fox must feel with the hounds behind it. I wasn't human any more, not really—just a frightened animal desperate to escape the men with guns.

Animals don't think: they act. I doubt if they feel fear, not in the way we usually mean the word. Feeling something, anything, is one of those little luxuries you need time for. We didn't have the time. We were too busy trying to escape. I was terrified of course, but it hardly counted because I couldn't spare a moment to think about it, to say "I am terrified" to myself. Someone should teach huntsmen the meaning of this kind of fear. If they're so keen on hunting, why don't they take it in turns to hunt each other? That would give them a whole new slant on blood sports.

Blood was pouring down my face. Some of it found its way into my mouth, and it tasted warm and salty. When the petrol tank went up, I'd been thrown against what felt like stonework—the foundations of a partition wall, perhaps. On the other hand, the cut might have been caused by thorns. Or both.

I followed Smith. Her shirt was a grey smudge ahead. Despite the fact her hands were tied, she was making better progress than me. Maybe it was because she's smaller and nippier or maybe she was even more scared. I figured we must be in what had once been a huge semi-basement that had probably extended beneath the whole house. Among the foliage were the remains of walls and doorways. Pillars like stone trees shot up to where the roof had been. I think the floor was flagged but it was carpeted with dead leaves and broken glass. The glass crunched underfoot.

Once I looked up and saw a charcoal sky far above an

anarchic tangle of branches. We staggered and scrambled and wriggled. Trees reared out of the gloom; the undergrowth snatched at our feet.

It was never entirely dark. In fact, the further we went, the better I could see. The security lamps around the house provided a sort of background lighting and my eyes were no longer dazzled by the prison-camp glare of the yard.

We were making a hell of a lot of noise. There is no way you can move through a dense mass of vegetation in silence, and we weren't even trying. Every now and then, I listened for sounds of pursuit. I heard nothing at all, and somehow that was worse than hearing footsteps.

After a while the going got easier—or rather slightly less difficult. I think we must have stumbled on an animal's run. A fox's, perhaps. I reckoned we were swinging to the left—in other words away from the drive and towards the back of the house.

Smith vanished through another doorway. This one still had its lintel but had lost its door. Just before I reached it, she gave a yell. I went after her. Suddenly the ground beneath my feet was no longer there.

I fell forwards into darkness. For one sickening instant I thought we'd fallen into a well. I waited for the splash that would mean Smith had hit water.

Then came a series of blows—on my upper arm, my ribs, my thigh and my knee. The air whooshed out of my lungs. My head thudded into something that was almost comfortable and surprisingly warm.

At least I'd stopped falling. The jolt seemed to have knocked some of the panic out of me. I was lying in a painful diagonal on what felt like a row of bruises. My neck was twisted. Only my head felt halfway tolerable. Then I had a jolt of a different kind when I realized that Smith had made that fall with her hands tied behind her back.

"Smith?" I croaked.

I heard a moan. Simultaneously I realized that I was lying on a flight of steps. The angles between the treads and risers were digging at regular intervals into my body. The air was cooler here and it smelled dank. The inky-black darkness suggested that we were enclosed by a roof and walls. A cellar of some sort?

I tried again. "Where are you?"

"Under your head," Smith said.

"What?"

"You're using my leg as a pillow."

Her voice was low and sort of thin, as if she were convalescing from a long and serious illness. I levered myself away from her and slithered down the steps. She groaned, and the darkness rustled. There were no sounds of pursuit. For all I knew we'd fallen through a black hole into another world where we were the only inhabitants. I sat on the bottom step and waved my arm in front of me. My fingers brushed warm skin.

Smith let out a squeal.

"It's only me."

"God, I thought it was a rat," she said.

"You're worrying about rats at a time like this?"

She said nothing.

"All right," I went on, realizing too late that rats were a lot more manageable than the rest of our problems. "So it was a stupid question. Are you okay?"

"No. But I'll live. Fifty per cent of me had a soft landing—feels like a pile of sacks. What about you?"

"Well, you know." I thought about cataloguing my various aches and pains but decided against it. "Routine wear and tear. Let me try and untie your hands."

She turned over and lay on her belly. The parcel tape had been wound tightly round her wrists. Luckily for her, they'd wound it over the cuffs of her shirt. I found the end of the tape and tried to peel it back. But my nails were short and my fingers were slippery with sweat and blood. I pulled about an inch up and then the tape split and I had to start all over again. This time I used my teeth and tried to gnaw through it. Take it from me: chewing through several layers of heavy-duty parcel tape in the darkness may sound a plausible thing to do; in practice it's impossible.

"I don't want to seem ungrateful," Smith hissed, "but that's the third time you've bitten me."

"I'll try and find something to cut it with."

"Don't go far."

For the first time there was an edge of panic in her voice.

"I won't." I eased myself up and my body groaned.

"Keep talking, Chris, okay?"

"I think we're in some kind of cellar," I said as I circled round her with my arms outstretched. It occurred to me that Smith, who had travelled here in the bottom of the VW camper, would know very little about our surroundings. "This is Biercetown House, you know. But the house itself is a ruin and the research laboratory is in the outbuildings . . . What is this? Feels like some kind of lawnmower . . . " I knocked into something hard, which scraped across the stone-flagged floor. "And this is definitely a wheelbarrow. If you ask me, we've found the Kinahans' garden shed. And – "

"How far are we from the road?"

"Miles. We're in the middle of a private park: there's barbed wire everywhere and lots of little security lamps all over the place. Hey—I've found some forks and spades." One of the spades had earth on its blade, and the earth was still damp. "There's a sort of table or workbench here . . . "

I looked—or rather felt—a little further and found a pair of shears. The blades were rough with rust but they still had an edge to them. I took them back to Smith and carried on talking.

"The cops are coming soon. The security guards are meant to make two-hourly phone checks. All we need to do is keep our heads down."

I knelt beside her and managed to get one of the blades of the shears between her wrists. I tried to cut the tape by bringing the blades gently together, but the shears weren't sharp enough.

"Put a bit of muscle into it," Smith said.

"I don't want to cut off your thumb by mistake."

"Yeah. I don't want tetanus on top of rabies."

"Charming," I said.

The fact she'd managed to make a joke made me feel a whole lot happier. I used one blade of the shears as a saw. I knew it must be hurting her—the sides of the blade were rubbing against her wrists. I wanted to hurry but I forced myself to saw slowly to and fro.

"It's working," she said. "I felt it give."

She flexed her wrists and the tape finally gave way. With a groan that was part-pain and part-relief, she rolled over and sat up. Her hands were numb, so I peeled the remains of the tape away from her wrists. I sat down beside her on the pile of sacks and tried to rub some life into her fingers.

"Listen," Smith whispered.

We listened. Something pitter-pattered away on the edge of my range of hearing: a small animal, perhaps, just as scared as we were. An owl hooted. A dog with a broken heart was yapping in the distance. Through the doorway came a surging sound like static ebbing and flowing at low volume: the wind moving through the trees.

"There's nothing to hear," I murmured. "Nothing that matters."

"So what are they doing?" Smith said.

I shrugged in the darkness. Priming their precious baby? Liberating the animals? Making themselves scarce? Or just waiting to spring a trap on us?

"I don't like this, Chris: I feel trapped."

"Maybe they've got more important things to do than chase after us."

"You want to bet on it?"

"I'm not in a betting mood."

"I don't like the dark. Never did."

She touched my leg. I took her hand. Don't get me

wrong: it wasn't a big romantic moment. We sat there listening for a moment or two.

"How come you're here?" she said at last.

"At Biercetown House? I thought you were here, and I thought I'd find a phone. But Eddy cut the lines. So I strolled up to the yard to look for you. I just happened to be in the Nissan when you all turned up."

"Cut it out, Dalham," she said. "Modesty doesn't suit you."

"I'm not really modest," I said modestly. "Just stupid."

"Thank God. They were going to kill us."

I couldn't think of anything to say to that. Twice before Smith and I had been close to death. But it isn't something you get used to. If anything, it gets worse the more it happens. Cats only have nine lives, you think: how many have I got?

"It seems to be getting darker," she said; and her fingers wriggled in my hand.

"No," I said. "Look, there's light coming through the doorway."

"Call that light? Look, if they're storing tools in here, there must be another way in, right? No one's going to bring a lawnmower the same way that we came."

She got up and pulled me after her. Her fingers dug into my arm as if she were afraid of losing me. I knew it was nothing personal. She was so scared of the dark she would have snuggled up to Dracula himself. My dad's the same—he has to sleep with the light on, and he sometimes dreams of being buried alive.

We zig-zagged slowly into the darkness, away from the steps and the doorway.

I told Smith about the fresh earth on the spade, which supported the theory that there was another way into this place. We found the lawnmower, the wheelbarrow and the workbench. Beyond that was a damp wall of unplastered stone. I got up on the bench and felt the roof. It curved gently away from me.

"Stone or brick ceiling," I said casually.

In my mind I heard the bomb going off and heard the roar of tons of masonry falling. I had the sense not to mention it to Smith.

We moved along the wall and found a door. The hinges were moist with oil. Both of us got very excited. Smith slowly pushed up the latch and pulled the door open.

Beyond it was more darkness. I felt as if we could spend the rest of our lives wandering through the bowels of the earth. Smith caught her breath. I guessed she was on the edge of tears. To be honest, I wasn't far away from tears myself.

"We could go back," I said. "Try to get out through the house."

"No. All those lights. We'd make a lot of noise. And what happens when the bomb goes up?"

So we pushed on. Hand in hand we went into the new darkness. By now I'd lost all sense of direction.

"In mazes," I said, "they say the way to get out is always to turn left. Or is it right? I suppose it comes to the same thing. I – "

I ran into another wall. Smith ran into me.

"Okay," I said, trying to sound masterful, cool-headed and constructive. "I suggest we turn left. And we go on turning left whenever we can't go straight on."

"You can suit yourself," Smith said. "Personally I'm turning right." Her voice wobbled, and she added in a rush: "Chris, there's light over there. Behind you."

She yelped with joy and buried her face in my shoulder. I turned and stared. I wasn't sure but the darkness looked a little lighter over there.

Smith broke away from me. I grabbed her arm and followed. We reached a door that was a few inches ajar. As Smith opened it, the light grew and became an uncurtained window. There was another window a few feet away. And between them pencil-thin lines of light marked the jambs and lintel of a door.

"Now look at that," Smith said.

We stood at the nearest window and looked out. The glass was filthy with dirt and old cobwebs. The light came from a row of security lamps outside. The window was set back in a grassy alcove between high stone walls. A gravel path crossed the mouth of the alcove. Beyond the path was a level area that had once been a lawn and was now a hayfield.

"I haven't seen this before," I whispered. "We must be at the back of the house."

"Come on."

"Wait. Maybe we're better off here."

"If they find us here, we're trapped. I don't want to sit waiting for trouble. Besides, it's dark."

I thought about what being buried alive would be like. It depended on where they sited the bomb, how big it was, how strong the ruins were. I shrugged. "Okay, then."

"Across that field and as far away as we can?"

I nodded.

Smith tried the door. "Hell, it's locked."

Hardly surprising that they'd lock even the garden shed at Biercetown House. I took a look at one of the windows. It was a casement. The handle squeaked as I moved it up. The hinges squealed as I pushed the window open.

I gave Smith a leg up. A moment later, we were both outside. The air smelled fresh and sweet and I felt euphoric. Feeling euphoric generally means you're about to do something stupid.

She gave me a smile and I guessed she was feeling even crazier than me. "Bet you can't jump the path," she said.

Before I could stop her, she was off, from 0 to 60 in two seconds. She sprinted silently down the grass. From somewhere she found the energy to clear the path in a single leap. I was already lumbering after her.

As she landed, she turned her head to the left. She landed, stumbled a few paces and dived flat on her face.

In consequence I bungled my take-off and landed with

one foot on the gravel. I plunged after her, deep into the long wet grass. I wriggled down, trying to keep as flat as possible.

We were at the back of Biercetown House. On our left was a brightly-lit jumble of single-storey buildings.

"The animal house?" Smith muttered.

The buildings were a tacky, utilitarian collection—very different from the rest of the research laboratory. They were connected by a sort of covered walkway to a modern block that was joined on to the end of the old house itself. I recognized the roofline: it was the back of the new building I'd seen from the stableyard.

Every window was alight. Together with the security lamps, that made far too much light for comfort. I could see Smith's face quite clearly. She looked terrible—smeared with dirt and perhaps soot from the fire. I felt horribly exposed. I once saw a guy running down Tottenham Court Road without his trousers on. Now I knew how he must have been feeling.

I turned my head a few degrees and stared up at the ruins of the mansion. It was set high above us on a stone-faced terrace. The back wall of the house was in far worse condition than the front. It looked like the bomb had already gone off. All the place needed was a few vampires and it would have been really homely.

But the terrace was still sound. I guessed that we'd fallen into a range of cellars beneath it. If we could have seen it from the air, the terrace would have looked like a capital E. A balustrade ran along the top, ending in a path that curved up to the block of offices. The centre bar of the E was formed by a massive flight of steps, with a pair of urns at the top and another at the bottom.

The window we had come through was recessed in one of the alcoves on either side of the steps. That was why we hadn't been able to see the lights of the animal house.

"It's no problem," Smith whispered. "They can't see us."

"You're assuming they're all inside," I pointed out.

"We'll listen and count to fifty. Then we make a break for it."

"Okay," I said.

Anything for a quiet life. Besides I didn't have a better idea. We'd run through the zone of light into the darkness. I just hoped we could cope with any nasty surprises the landscape had in store for us.

Smith counted very slowly. "Ten," she murmured after what seemed like several minutes. "Twenty . . . Thirty . . . Forty . . . "

But she never reached fifty.

"Help!" someone yelled. "Please help!"

Three linked figures were moving slowly along the terrace in the direction of the animal house. All they had to do was look to their right, over the balustrade, and they could hardly help but see us.

The nearer they got to the animal house, the better the light became. Finch and Eddy were marching steadily along. Between them, and facing the other way, was Gerald, his arms trapped by the men on either side of him.

I realized then why Heinrich hadn't bothered to hunt us down. Gerald was a more important quarry.

"Can't we talk about this?" Gerald said as they passed along the terrace directly above where we were lying. "If it's a question of money – "

"No, Gerald," said Eddy. "There's nothing left to say. You're going to give our baby a nice little cuddle."

CHAPTER TWELVE

"The baby," Smith muttered. "That means – "

"Yeah," I said. "You don't need to spell it out."

Eddy, Finch and Gerald disappeared through a door in the side of the walkway. Now was our chance to make a break, to run through the long grass to the wide open spaces of the park beyond. There was a whole world out there just waiting for us to hide in it.

"But they wouldn't," Smith went on. "Not really. They must have been just talking. A threat, right? Verbal bullying."

I wished I could agree. "Gerald's seen as much of them as we have," I said. "More—he spent a long time alone with Heinrich. And if they want to make an example of this place to frighten other scientists, if they want the publicity—well, who better to choose than the boss's son?"

"But it's so callous."

"They were going to kill you both in the yard. What's so different?"

"We got to do something," Smith said.

Her head was six inches away from mine. I tried to read the expression on her face. Gerald, I thought. Why couldn't he have come along a couple of minutes later? And I had the same sour feeling I'd had in Dublin this morning—when I'd tailed Smith and Gerald to find out if they were just good friends or something more romantic.

"Well, I guess *I* have to do something," Smith said. She used her arrogant voice, the one that's designed to make you feel knee-high to a woodlouse. "You can please yourself."

"Don't be stupid," I said coldly.

"Are you trying to tell me what to do?"

Before I could answer the door in the walkway opened. But there was no one there. I blinked. Something was moving. It looked as if an inch-high tide of thick white liquid was pouring through the doorway. The tide flowed on to the path and drained into the long grass on either side.

The flow petered out. Then Julia was standing in the doorway, her long brown hair swinging from side to side. She waved her arms high above her head and for an instant she looked almost impressive, like the high priestess of an ancient cult.

"Shoo, my little darlings!" she cried. "Shoo!"

Smith snorted softly in a mixture of laughter and relief. "She's liberating the white mice."

Julia vanished, leaving the door open. I wondered if she'd already freed the rats and rabbits to a short and nasty life in the wild. In a funny way I almost liked Julia. In contrast with her male colleagues, there was quite a lot to be said in her favour.

"Okay," I said. "What about Gerald then?"

"You're coming with me?"

"Strictly on humanitarian grounds. There are two technicians inside as well as him."

"I'd forgotten about them."

I thought she had. The girl was obviously obsessed with Gerald. I said, "We got to think this out properly before we move."

"Those guys are not going to blow themselves up," Smith said briskly. "So all we have to do is hide in or near the building, and nip inside when Heinrich leaves."

I felt ill. "You make it sound so simple."

"What about that corner by the door?"

She pointed to the angle between the walkway and the office block. It was certainly in shadow and conveniently close to the door. I cleared my throat and tried to think of a diplomatic way to frame my objections to her plan.

Just a few minor points: for example, if they found us in that corner, we'd have nowhere to run to; and if the bomb went off prematurely, the entire building would in all probability collapse on top of us.

It was too late. Before I could say a word, Smith had come to one of her unilateral decisions. She was up and running. Like a fool I followed her.

The ground rose sharply, sloping up to the level of the terrace. The grass was alive with white mice. They were doing a lot of squeaking—probably having a mass-meeting to try to work out why they had been expelled from their nice, warm, comfy cages. I do hope I didn't tread on any of them. Life's tough, I wanted to tell them, when you're out in the real world.

What happened in the next few seconds was like a swift descent to another, nastier level of the nightmare. I suppose it had its comic side but at the time I didn't feel like laughing.

To my astonishment, Smith swerved to the right when the ground levelled out. Instead of running into the darkened corner she put down her head and shot through the open door into the passage beyond.

I remember thinking that she must have cracked up. The strain had finally got to her. It must have got to me as well because I changed course to follow her.

As I swerved I saw why she'd changed her mind. The corner was already occupied. About thirty large white rats were having a lively conference about current affairs. Smith does not like rats. Nor do I. Sometimes you do the damnedest silly thing for the damnedest silly reasons.

I skidded to a halt, just inside the door. The strip lighting made me blink. The corridor was a bleak, echoing place with linoleum underfoot and puke-green paint on the walls. Smith looked filthy, like a chimney sweep who hadn't had a bath for months. No doubt I was in much the same condition, with added blood. I grabbed her arm, intending to brave the rats and haul her back outside.

The swing doors to our right began to open. Julia backed through, holding them open with her shoulders.

"Come to Mummy, darling," she cooed. "This way."

Smith jerked her arm away from me. She was looking not at Julia but at the open door behind us.

The white rats were moving in a purposeful body over the threshold. They'd obviously put the matter to the vote and decided that freedom was a poor exchange for three square meals a day and a really efficient central-heating system. They trotted towards us. Unlike us, they weren't a bit afraid. These were tame rats. They thought all humans were their friends.

Smith sort of gargled deep in her throat. She jumped sideways—away from the rats and away from Julia—and collided with another pair of swing doors. They swung open and she fell through.

What could I do? I followed her and closed the doors behind me.

We were in another corridor, far grander than the one we had just left. It ran through the office block in the direction of the yard. The walls were painted cream and decorated with architectural engravings. Facing us was another set of double doors—half-glazed, so you could see the corridor stretching away on the other side. On our right was a solid mahogany door with a brass-framed notice on it saying CONFERENCE ROOM. To the left, the corridor opened out into a sort of high-class waiting room.

"Go away!" Julia shrieked, presumably at the rats. "You can't come back—you're free!"

Pot plants and black leather armchairs were scattered over a blood-red carpet. Someone had arranged a selection of magazines and newspapers on the glass-topped table in front of a four-seater sofa. A filter coffee machine gleamed on top of a filing cabinet. The jug was empty, of course. It made me realize that I was hungry and thirsty. On the farther wall was another mahogany door, a few inches ajar. It had a matching brass-framed notice on it: THE DIRECTOR.

" . . . now be reasonable, Gerald," Heinrich was saying on the other side of the door. "What are you? Just another animal. Why should your life be any more important than all the animals your father has slaughtered? Look at it rationally. You will have a nice, clean, quick death. Many people would envy you, and so would many of your father's victims. And by dying in this way you will almost certainly make your father think twice before he kills again. You are dying that others may live. Few of us can tell ourselves that. It must be a great consolation."

The noise that followed was less than human. I once watched a couple of men load a bunch of pigs on a truck bound for the slaughterhouse: the pigs made a noise like that.

I nudged Smith and pointed to the sofa. It was at least a foot away from the wall and it had one of those overhanging backs. Smith nodded. We crawled between it and the wall. It could turn out to be more than a hiding-place, I thought: it might give us some shelter from the blast.

"We really should be going," Finch said.

Heinrich ignored him. "If we're lucky," he went on in a dreamy voice, "the explosion will bring down that wall behind you. It's a load-bearing wall, I think—the effect might be quite dramatic."

"For God's sake, look at the time," Eddy shouted. "The guards are meant to be phoning the cops in five minutes."

"As you wish." Heinrich sounded almost disappointed. "I'll go and see how Julia's getting on. Our very own St Francis, eh? I wonder if you two would start a little fire, just to add to the confusion. There's a fuel store in the old stables, the second door – "

"We haven't got the time," Eddy snapped.

Finch said, "What about the technicians?"

Heinrich sighed. "What about them?"

"We can't just leave them."

"Why not?"

"We'll have to leave them," Eddy said.

"No way." Finch must have opened the door: his voice was much louder. "They're not in the same category as young Kinahan. I'm going to move them."

"May I remind you – "

"I know you're the boss, Heinrich. I've heard that speech before. But I'm going to move them anyway, all right?"

Finch stomped across the waiting room and went through the swing doors on the left, the ones that led towards the yard. The other men followed him out of the director's office.

"I suppose he's got a point," Heinrich said. "One has to think of the public-relations angle."

"I'm going," Eddy said.

"Give me five minutes. Get the VW out of the way. The Nissan's useless. We'll have to use the Land Rover, I'm afraid. Check the fuel tank and get it facing the right way."

"Which gates are we going for?"

"The back ones, of course. The Garda will try the front entrance first, the one we came in by. Then we head for Newtown Mount Kennedy, switch cars and go our separate ways. There's nothing to worry about."

"Except the time," Eddy said.

"Don't do anything rash, will you?"

"What do you mean?"

"I mean that my friends in Frankfurt will be very worried if I don't come back. They will know who to blame. Think about it, Eddy. Think very carefully."

Hinges creaked, and silence settled over the waiting room. Smith moved forwards, digging one heel into my hand. We scrambled to our feet. Gerald was doing his imitation of a doomed pig, and believe me it was the reverse of funny. We went through the door marked DIRECTOR.

It led to a tiny anteroom with a desk, a typewriter, a computer and a wall full of filing cabinets. Stephen Kinahan had a secretary to insulate him from the outside world. Beyond the anteroom was his own office, a big, square room with a couple of sash windows, a high ceiling and fancy plasterwork. It looked much older than the rest of the office block—perhaps it was a leftover from the original Biercetown House.

There was an old-fashioned desk with a lot of drawers, two or three chairs and very little else. At right angles to the desk was a table with two useless telephones and a computer. An oriental carpet—geometrical swirls in dark reds and blues—covered two-thirds of the space; the rest was just varnished floorboards. The chair between the desk and the far wall had a high, carved back and wooden arms.

Gerald was sitting there. In his father's chair.

You could hardly see him for parcel tape. His arms and legs were strapped to the arms and legs of the chair. They'd wrapped more of the stuff round his mouth and over the bridge of his nose.

It was a miracle he was still able to breathe; they must have left a gap somewhere. His chest heaved up and down. His eyes poked out of his head like a pair of bright and bloodshot mega-marbles. What you could see of his skin was an unhealthy shade of purple, shining with sweat.

"Don't worry," Smith said. "We'll get you out of this. Just you – "

She stopped talking and she stopped moving. It was as if she were hypnotized. She was looking at the huge desk, and so was I.

The desk was built of oak, stained and polished to an almost golden sheen, and fitted with a green leather top. There were only two things on it: Heinrich's black briefcase and a shallow tray made of grey plastic. On the tray was a heap of what looked like fresh pink putty. I think it smelled faintly of marzipan but that may have been my imagination. There were a lot of wires, and what might have been the guts of a portable radio, battery included.

The contents of the tray didn't look in any way menacing. Nothing ticked. There wasn't a sign saying BOMB. In a way it was an oddly homely sight—the sort of thing you find in someone's toolshed; the sort of collection someone's kid brother assembles when no one's keeping an eye on him.

"We need something to cut the tape," I said. "Try the briefcase. Maybe they brought wire-cutters."

I went round the desk, tried one of the drawers and found a wodge of blotting paper. The next one down was full of stationery. Smith shook herself and opened the briefcase.

She said, "I'm sure if we took one of those wires out . . . "

Her voice died away.

"Which wire?" I said angrily. "For all we know we'd just short-circuit the timer."

"If we thought about it logically – "

"Cut it out, will you?"

This was not the moment for taking a learn-as-you-go course in bomb-disposal. In the fourth drawer down I found one of those masculine manicure sets you see in the stores around Christmas time. It included a pair of folding nail scissors. Gerald was grunting and trying to rock himself to and fro without much success. He smelled. Maybe I did too. Fear makes people smell bad.

"Sit still, you fool, or I'll cut you," I snarled. "I'll do the legs first, okay?"

The scissors were blunt and too small for my fingers. Gerald wouldn't stop twitching, which made the process slower than it might have been. I got the first leg free and he started kicking the desk.

"Don't kick!" I yelled. "You might set the bomb off."

That frightened him into temporary immobility. He

was still grunting like a demented pig and I wished he would stop.

I suddenly realized how vulnerable we were. "Watch the door," I said to Smith. "In fact you'd be more use out in the corridor."

"Sure," she said vaguely, looking up from the briefcase. "In a moment. This is important."

I would have argued but just then I managed to free the other leg. Gerald tried to stand up, chair and all. I pushed him down, none too gently, and he calmed down enough for me to slice through the tape that bound his left arm. I was getting the knack of it now and I freed the right arm in about three seconds flat.

"I'll leave the tape round the mouth," I told him. "I think you really need medical – "

Gerald didn't hang around to hear the rest of my advice or grunt his thanks. He belted round the desk and out of the door.

"Take a look at this," Smith said. "It's – "

"Later. Let's go."

She shut the briefcase. "Chris, will you listen to me?"
Crack!

For an instant I thought the bomb had gone up. My heart rolled over. Glass tinkled outside. Not the bomb: a gunshot. Someone screamed. People seemed to be running around all over the place, inside and out.

Eddy was crouching in the doorway of Kinahan's office. He had his hands wrapped round the butt of an automatic. The muzzle was pointing straight at me.

CHAPTER THIRTEEN

"I want both of you against that wall." The barrel of the gun twitched to the right. "Away from the desk. Nice and easy, nice and slow."

For a long moment neither Smith nor I obeyed. She was staring at the desk—at the briefcase and the contents of the grey tray. Her lips moved silently; I've seen people look like that when they're having trouble with mental arithmetic. Then she glanced at me and strolled to the wall opposite the windows. Yes—she strolled, as if she had all the time in the world and nothing unpleasant on her mind. She leaned her back against the wall and folded her arms.

"You're making a big mistake," she said. "Let me tell you something. If you – "

"And you,' Eddy said to me.

"Anything you say." I walked round the desk and joined Smith. My legs wobbled and so did my voice. "But you can't afford to kill us, you know."

Eddy glanced at his watch and then at the grey tray on the desk. That made me nervous. He didn't ask me what I meant, not then—which in a way was just as well. I didn't have any reasons to give him. I just wanted to keep him talking. I assumed that Smith was trying to do the same.

"I want to tell you something," she said.

"I don't want to hear," Eddy said in a voice that wasn't much more than a whisper.

He took a deep breath and steadied his back against the door jamb. The muzzle panned from me to Smith and back again.

I looked at Eddy and he looked at me. His face was full of lines—the eyes narrowed, the mouth drawn back and the nostrils flared. He was psyching himself up for something. I knew what it was.

He'd appointed himself as a one-man firing squad.

"Do you want us to help you or not?" I said. I was scared witless but I think I just sounded irritable and perhaps a bit short of breath.

Eddy frowned.

Finch loomed up behind him. "What's all this?"

It would be an understatement to say that I was glad to see him. I knew that Finch was a nasty piece of work, for all that he looked like a trainee Santa Claus. But he lacked something that Eddy had. He didn't have quite the same compulsion to be ruthless.

The tension flowed out of Eddy's body. He straightened up and said, "I found these two here. They must have freed young Kinahan. Where is he? Did you get him?"

Finch shook his head and his beard wagged from side to side. "I tried to catch him but he was going like a bat out of hell." He waved his thumb over his shoulder. "There's a side door out into the park. He went through and vanished."

"You should have gone after him."

"There wasn't time." Finch, too, looked at his watch. "This is a right cock-up. Does Heinrich know?"

"I haven't seen him."

"Maybe he didn't hear, not if he's still in the animal house. All those doors act as sound barriers."

By now I'd worked out more or less what must have happened. Gerald had burst out of the office probably at the very moment when Eddy was coming down the corridor from the yard. Perhaps Finch, having taken the technicians outside, was with him. One of them had fired at Gerald, but missed. Eddy came to find out what was happening in here while Finch went after Gerald.

And Finch had let him get away. Intentionally? I wondered if, when it came to the crunch, Finch had less enthusiasm for murder than the others.

"These two will do just as well," Eddy said, and his voice sounded thicker, the words less distinct. He nodded at Smith. "Her mother's one of Kinahan's clients."

"It might be counter-productive," Finch pointed out. "I mean we need publicity, but not bad publicity."

"All publicity is good publicity," Eddy said; and he made it sound like a slogan he'd just invented.

Finch looked at his watch again. Eddy looked at his. Time was running out for all of us. They had the advantage over us. They had watches and they knew when the bomb was going up. From the moment they'd snatched us at the Warehouse and taken our watches, Smith and I had lived in a sort of limbo outside time.

"Excuse me," Smith said. "I'd like to say something."

"Shut your trap," Eddy shouted. He took a breath of air and said to Finch, "What are you waiting for? Tie them up."

"We've run out of parcel tape," Finch said.

"Oh my God. Talk about bloody amateurs. Find something else."

"We haven't got time."

There it was again—*time*.

"All right—so we shoot them first."

Finch wrinkled his nose but didn't reply.

"Come on," Eddy said, his voice rising. "We can't stay here all night. We've got to make up our minds."

"Where the hell is Heinrich?"

"If you shoot us," I said loudly, "you'll never find the camera."

That threw them. I think they'd have felt much the same way if one of the chairs had said something to them.

Finch turned to me, and I think he was glad I'd offered him a diversion. "What camera?"

"My camera."

They both looked blank.

"Heinrich nicked it from me this morning—in Dublin. I found it in the Nissan."

"Ignore him," Eddy said. "It's a delaying tactic."

"Heinrich had left the film in," I went on. "So I took two more shots from the back of the car. When the four of you were in the yard with Smith and Gerald. Remember?"

"There wasn't enough light," Eddy snapped. "And we'd have noticed if you'd used flash."

"I was using high-speed film," I lied. "1250 ASA. There was plenty of light for that."

Finch came a step nearer, and I saw that he too had a gun in his hand. At least it was pointing at the floor. "What are you trying to tell us?"

"There are three shots on that film. The one of Heinrich that I took this morning. One of you and one of Eddy. Good ones, too. I know what I'm doing with a camera."

As I was talking, in a confident voice that I hardly recognized as my own, it occurred to me that it was highly improbable that there were any negative images on the film. True, Heinrich had left the film in the camera. But he wasn't a fool and he wouldn't have left the evidence lying around. If I'd been in a hurry as he was, I'd have simply opened the back of the camera and exposed the whole film.

"All this is irrelevant," Eddy said. "Gerald Kinahan can describe us. What's the difference?"

"There's a big difference. A good photo's worth twenty descriptions. And Gerald never saw Heinrich's face—but my camera did. When the cops get here, they'll go through the whole place, every square inch. Sooner or later they'll find it."

Finch sneaked yet another look at his watch. "Where is it then? Still in the car?"

I shook my head. "It's in those ruins. I hid it there. You'll never find it in a month of Sundays. But I'm offering you a deal."

"He's bluffing," Eddy said. A muscle in his left eyelid had begun to twitch. He kept winking at us.

"It won't hurt to hear what he's got to say." Finch waved his gun at me. "But hurry."

"You let Smith go. She can't do you any harm, not now. Once she's outside and out of sight, I'll take you to where I left the camera."

"No deal," Finch said. "Too risky."

Eddy nodded. "We'd better get Heinrich in on this."

"If I were you," Smith said softly, "I'd take a look inside that briefcase first."

"Now *she's* trying to stall," Eddy said, winking furiously. "I've had enough of this."

"I thought you'd like to know who you're working for. Heinrich's been taking you for a ride." Smith paused for a second. "Didn't you notice it was a *leather* briefcase?"

Something Julia had said to me—hours before, when we were alone at the cottage—floated into my mind: *Everything we swallow, everything we wear, everything we touch* . . . Surely an animal rights activist would try to avoid leather?

Finch strode up to the desk and snapped open the catches on the briefcase. He lifted the lid. I glimpsed something brown and furry inside the case. He recoiled.

"It's okay," Smith said in a soothing voice. "It's only Heinrich's false beard."

Finch lifted out the contents, one by one, keeping up a rapid running commentary. There was a Swiss passport in the name of Herr Doktor Martin Somebody. Two fat wads of currency—Irish punts and Deutschmarks. A spare battery. Three clips of ammunition. A full-length raincoat in green, lightweight nylon, which had been rolled up and tucked inside a black beret. A pair of glasses with heavy black rims and slightly-tinted lenses. A photograph of Smith, which Eddy, Finch and Julia had used to identify her at the Warehouse this evening. A safe-deposit receipt from the Bandon Arms Hotel in County Cork. A set of car keys with a rental firm's logo on the tag.

"What are you going on about?" Eddy said. "There's nothing out of the ordinary."

It depended, I supposed, what you meant by "ordinary".

"Look at that photograph," Smith said.

Finch obediently held it up. It was a colour shot of Smith on 10" by 8" paper. She was walking down a London street; you could tell it was in London because there was a red pillar box on the corner of the road.

"What's so odd about that?" Eddy said.

"Heinrich didn't have a shot of Gerald for you to use," Smith said. "And he wasn't going to do anything as risky as kidnapping us himself. He likes you guys to take the risks around here—haven't you noticed? So he popped out with a Polaroid this morning to try and get a picture. He probably tailed us into Dublin from Bray Road South. Didn't it strike you as strange that he already had a photo of me—taken in England, a real professional job? You were meant to be targeting the Kinahans, not me. But the photo suggests that Heinrich saw it the other way round, that Gerald was a sort of afterthought."

"You're just trying to stir it," Eddy said.

"You think so? Why don't you take a look at the files at the bottom of the briefcase?"

Finch fanned them out on the desk. They were looseleaf purple folders with black plastic spines. On the front of each was BIERCETOWN HOUSE SCIENTIFIC ESTABLISHMENT embossed in gold above a rectangular window that showed the title-page of the documents inside.

"'Product Range H8, (a) to (g),'" Finch read out. He glanced at Eddy. "'Client Name: Weyburn Cosmetics.'"

"My mother," Smith said, "as you probably know, is Astrid Weyburn. Right now she's staying with the Kinahans."

"Are they all Weyburn Cosmetics files?" Eddy said.

Finch nodded. He opened one of them and looked at the table of contents. "Nasty. These are the findings. They do LD50 tests here."

Eddy stuck out his jaw. "Maybe Heinrich's group is planning to put pressure on the US cosmetics industry. Okay, he didn't mention it to us, but he didn't need to, did he? It's not suspicious."

"There's a lot he didn't mention. Look in the pocket in the lid. You'll find a card for a restaurant called Venger's. You know it? It's in Upper Leeson Street, Dublin. The card had got snagged in the bottom of the pocket. There's something written on the back."

Finch looked at Eddy. "It says 'Phone M. G. Friday 21.45'. Looks like Heinrich's writing. Hard to be sure."

"Yesterday was Friday," Smith said. "Last night my mother and Stephen Kinahan had dinner at Venger's with a guy called Michel Gill. He's a heavyweight in Vichy-White-Duloz. You've maybe heard of them?"

"European-based multi-national," Finch said. "Pharmaceuticals, cosmetics, medical appliances—that sort of thing. We've got their UK division down as a possible target for next year's offensive."

"Heinrich called someone last night at 9.45. Am I right?"

Eddy winked. Finch said nothing.

"Now you know who it was," Smith said. "Michel Gill. It's not hard to figure out why."

Finch dropped the card. It fluttered down to the desk and lay there, midway between the briefcase and bomb.

"You could have planted that card," Eddy said. He didn't sound convinced by the theory.

Smith ignored him altogether. "My mother's planning to break into the European market with a new product range. That's what Kinahan's testing for her. Vichy-White-Duloz aren't looking forward to the competition—they reckon it could cost them a big slice of the market. So they offered to buy a controlling share of Weyburn Cosmetics. My mother gave Michel Gill the final no last night. But it looks like VWD were expecting that, and they'd already lined up an alternative strategy."

"You mean they'd already lined up Heinrich?" Finch was looking very ugly. "And he'd already lined up us?"

"You got a better explanation?" Smith said. "They play rough in the cosmetics industry."

"But Kinahan's the target here."

"For you, maybe. Not for Heinrich. He's here to delay the Weyburn tests and do a little industrial espionage. That means the launch will have to be postponed—and also that the whole world will know that Weyburn Cosmetics runs tests on animals. And there's a personal angle, too—he's trying to frighten my mother off by hitting at me and the Kinahans. Oh, and don't forget the financial side: if the launch is delayed, or maybe cancelled, my mother's backers are going to get very worried about their investment. If they call in their loans, the company will crash."

"Hell of a risk for VWD to take." Finch began to shovel Heinrich's belongings into the briefcase. "If you're right, that is. And a lot of money, too."

Smith shook her head. "This way works out a whole lot cheaper than buying into my mother's company. And where's the risk? They don't get their hands dirty. Heinrich sees to all that, doesn't he? And *he* doesn't get his hands dirty either, or not so that it matters. He doesn't need to. The People for Animals Faction is doing most of the work for him. And whatever happens, you guys are going to get all the blame."

Eddy's face was full of lines again. He was psyching himself up. The other eye started blinking too. I measured the distance to the door. He looked at Finch.

"I'm going to – "

But we never found out what Eddy planned to do. Because at that moment there was an almighty crash in the direction of the waiting room.

"Walkies!" Julia yelled. "This way!"

A couple of seconds later a horde of beagles surged into Kinahan's office.

CHAPTER FOURTEEN

The beagles were deliriously happy to meet us. They milled around the office, trying to trip us up and trying to lick everyone's hand at once.

"Get off me," Eddy screeched, and he sounded frightened. He backed himself against the wall and waved his arms about, which made them even more excited than before.

The dogs were a sociable lot with wagging tails and wet noses. In their way they were quite a good advertisement for animal testing—they obviously liked humans; none of them had two heads or five legs; and there wasn't a cancerous growth in sight. Apart from the sheer quantity of them, they were just like ordinary dogs. Their normality was eerie.

Julia peered into the room, frowning a little when she saw the four of us. I realized that she could have very little idea what was happening. She'd missed all the excitement. Since Smith and I had escaped from the yard, she had been concentrating on the animal house.

"Well, come on," she said. "Help me get them out."

"What the hell are you doing?" Eddy said with all the unpleasantness he could manage.

You could tell by the manic gleam in her eyes that Julia was a woman with a mission. At present she wasn't frightened of anyone and she wasn't particularly interested in what we humans had been doing.

"We've got to let the dogs out this way, through the offices and into the yard," she said. "It's obvious, isn't it?"

"What is?" Finch asked.

"If we let them out at the back, they'll chase the rats."

105

"Where's Heinrich?"

"He's still in the animal house." She flushed with anger. "I tried to get him to help, but he wouldn't. As if *anything* could be more important than these poor dogs."

One of the poor dogs was trying to climb up her leg. She patted its head absent-mindedly.

"So what's he doing?" Eddy said.

"Collecting things. Computer discs and files. He's smashed a few instruments. He said he wouldn't be long."

"Julia," Finch said, "Heinrich's working for the enemy. He doesn't give a damn about us and the animals. We're going to leave without him."

Beside me, Smith let out her breath. I shared her relief. Finch had decided to believe her. Surely that would change everything? They were against Heinrich now, not us.

"I never liked him," Julia said. She didn't sound surprised. I think her head was so full of the beagles that it didn't have room for much else. "Please help me get the dogs out."

Finch picked up the briefcase and moved away from the desk. Julia caught sight of the grey plastic tray.

"Is that the–?"

"The baby?" Finch said. "Yes, and that's another reason why we haven't much time. Okay, let's get the dogs out. All of us will help." He looked at Smith and me. "You as well."

At least Finch was trying to be consistent. Like Julia, he cared about what happened to the animals.

Julia, Eddy and Smith led the way. "Walkies!" Julia called. Finch and I herded the dogs after them.

Barking happily, the beagles scrambled through the doorway, across the secretary's room and into the waiting room beyond. The doors to the animal house were closed. Julia turned left, in the opposite direction, and went through another pair of swing doors. The dogs gambolled after her, jostling each other as they raced down the thickly-carpeted corridor. There were doors on either side. All but one of them was closed.

Finch and I walked behind with the beagle rearguard— half a dozen dogs that weren't in quite as much of a hurry as the rest. One of them tried to slip off to explore what lay beyond the half-open door. I grabbed his collar and hauled him back. I glimpsed a metal tag on the collar. Instead of a name, this dog had a number: 505.

505 didn't seem to mind my re-routeing him. He licked my hand and charged after the others.

As we walked, Finch kept glancing back through the open doors.

"What happens if Heinrich comes out?" I said.

"None of your business."

"Are you going to let us go?"

Finch didn't bother to reply. I couldn't figure him out. He'd gone to a lot of trouble to make sure that the captured technicians didn't go up with the bomb. He cared about the dogs. He acted as a brake on Eddy's more anti-social activities. Yet Finch had seemed perfectly happy for Gerald to be blown into little pieces. He was a terrorist, a man who killed for a cause. I had an unpleasant suspicion that he hadn't finished with us.

I was pretty sure that he would kill us if he felt it was necessary; and he would do it efficiently, even if he did it reluctantly. He might think that killing Smith would be good for business: as an object lesson for Astrid Weyburn and Stephen Kinahan.

We reached another pair of swing doors. The corridor swung right. A few yards on was another set of doors. Then the corridor split into two: one branch carried on down the length of the building; the other led through yet another pair of doors to the yard. I had to restrain 505 from battering his way through the wrong set of doors; he was the sort of dog who likes to make his own decisions.

The others were already outside. The big, harshly-lit

yard was just as we'd left it: the VW camper was standing with its doors open; beyond it was the Land Rover; and the blackened wreck of the Nissan was rammed against the wall of the ruined house; Eddy's axe was still lying on the gravel. I joined Smith, who was leaning against one of the technicians' cars.

"Don't upset them," she murmured.

The dogs were going crazy at the thought of some unscheduled night-time exercise in the open air. Most of them were cocking their legs to assert their territorial rights. There were fewer of them than I'd thought. When they were moving rapidly in a confined space, they'd looked like an army. Now—seeing them spread out in the yard—I reckoned there were only fifty or sixty of them.

"Will the dogs be safe here?" Julia asked Finch.

I guessed she meant when the bomb went up.

"Probably. But it'd be safer still to get them right outside the yard."

Julia began to run towards the archway. She yelled at the dogs and most of them followed her.

"Where did you put the technicians?" Eddy said.

"In one of the rooms over there." Finch pointed at the far right-hand corner of the yard, at the end of the old stable range that linked the new building to the wall with the archway at the front. "They'll be okay. I want you to stay here and watch for Heinrich."

Eddy licked his lips. "And if he comes?"

"Don't hang about. Shoot on sight."

"But what if he doesn't come? We can't let him get away with this."

"We shan't," Finch said. "We're going to leave him." He tapped the briefcase with the barrel of his gun. "He won't get far without this. Especially if he hasn't got transport. And I'm going to make very sure he hasn't."

"He might talk to the cops."

"There's not a lot he can say. He doesn't know where we're going. He doesn't know our real names."

Eddy blinked at Smith and me. "What about–?"

"I want that camera," Finch said.

"And then?"

Finch smiled at us. "If they cooperate, we'll let them go. They'll be useful—they can tell the cops about Heinrich."

"Are you sure?"

"Trust me," Finch said, still smiling.

I couldn't work out whether he was telling the truth or just playing us along. I didn't trust those jolly smiles. On the one hand the operation had already been a success—from PAF's viewpoint, that is: after all the publicity, Biercetown House Scientific Establishment would never be the same again. On the other hand, Smith and I knew what Eddy and Finch looked like; to some extent we had to be a security risk.

Both Eddy and Finch consulted their watches.

"When's the bomb going up?" I asked.

Finch shook his head. "You don't need to know that. Go and get the camera."

"He might run away," Eddy said.

"No, he won't. Not if the girl's here."

Finch was a psychologist.

"Will you let Smith go?" I said.

"When you come back with the camera."

"No. Now."

"Look, boy." Finch raised the gun and sighted down the barrel at Smith. "Don't argue. We haven't time for it."

I didn't argue. I ran across the yard towards the Nissan and the steps that led into the ruin.

"I'd hurry if I were you," Finch called after me. "I wouldn't like to be trapped in that house when the bomb goes up."

I passed the black Land Rover, ran round the Nissan and plunged down the steps to the doorway. I heard feet pattering after me. One of the beagles had decided to come along for the ride.

"Go away," I yelled at him.

He barked at me, pretending to be hostile and really inviting me to play a game with him. I ignored him.

Being inside that house was like being underwater—on the bottom of the ocean, among a forest of weeds; too deep for the light to penetrate. I needed time to let my eyes adjust to the light. And of course time was one of the many things I didn't have.

I searched blindly for the camera. I knew it couldn't be far from the doorway. When its strap broke, the Zeiss had trapped itself behind a fallen branch.

From the yard came the sound of breaking glass.

The sudden violence of it tipped me over the edge. I panicked and ran back to the doorway. I climbed up a couple of steps and peered under the Nissan. I was just in time to see Finch swinging the axe against the windscreen of the second of the technicians' cars. He turned to Smith.

"Get the keys out of the camper," he said. "Drop them down the drain near the Land Rover."

Eddy was crouching by the doorway, covering the corridor. I couldn't see Julia but I could hear her shouting at the dogs.

"Run!" Finch shouted at Smith.

The panic bit deeper. I remembered the bomb, not that I'd really forgotten it. I stumbled back inside the ruins. Kinahan's office wasn't far from where I was standing. I could imagine all too well the effect of a bomb blast on what was left of Biercetown House.

I got on my hands and knees and scrabbled among the rubble, the weeds, the dead leaves. A shard of broken glass sliced into my hand. I found a lot more nettles. The camera could be anywhere. The whole place looked unfamiliar. Last time I'd passed through here, I'd been in too much of a hurry to take note of the scenery.

The beagle, yapping with excitement, had joined in the hunt. It kept getting in my way.

"Get out of here, you fool," I said.

The axe smashed into another windscreen—the VW's?

The dog butted me playfully. I hooked a thumb round his collar and tried to pull him off. Just inside the doorway the light was quite good: I could read the serial number on his brass tag.

505 licked my face. 505—what a name for an animal. My mind skipped sideways for one split second. I remembered two other animals with stupid names—a couple of cats called Pseud and Alias. That's another story. But if it hadn't been for Pseud and Alias, I would never have met Smith. If it hadn't been for them, I wouldn't have been here.

For some illogical reason that made me feel a little better. My panic didn't vanish but it subsided to more manageable proportions. Cameras don't disappear from the face of the earth. All I had to do was search methodically and I'd find it—sooner or later; preferably sooner.

"505," I said in what I hoped was a voice of command. "Camera. Find. Good boy."

I went on crawling, sweeping the ground with my outstretched hands, for what seemed like years and was probably a couple of minutes. 505 licked my hand when he could reach it; either he liked the taste of fresh blood or he was trying to administer first aid.

At the end of a small eternity I caught sight of the camera. It was much nearer the doorway than I'd expected. The light glinted on its metal trim. I should have been able to find it in seconds.

I picked it up. 505 pranced around, waving his tail—in fact generally behaving as though he'd found it for me. As I walked up the steps with the dog at my heels, I turned the camera over to open the back. Finch could have the film. I hoped he'd let me keep the Zeiss. I feel only half a person without a camera.

The back was a little loose; the catch hadn't engaged

properly. It confirmed what I'd already suspected: that Heinrich had opened the camera to expose the film. The film was still inside. But I didn't have time to take it out.

By now my head was above ground level. The brightness of the light made me feel vulnerable. I stopped climbing and glanced around the yard. The first person I saw was Smith.

She was quite close to me—walking along the side of the Land Rover with the briefcase in her hand; I guessed that Finch had told her to put it inside. She didn't see me—not then.

Finch was in the middle of the yard, crouching over the drain. He was feeding what looked like wires into it—perhaps the H/T leads from the VW and technicians' cars.

I looked under the Nissan and there was Eddy, still waiting at the doorway with his gun in both hands.

Julia was standing near the wheeled dustbins just inside the archway. She was trying to persuade half a dozen beagles that they would be happier elsewhere. They wanted to stay with her.

Smith looked across at the Nissan and saw me. I knew that we had a chance to escape, and I wondered if she'd seen it too. Finch and Eddy were busy. We could make a break for it through the ruins and hope that the bomb didn't go off while we were inside.

But I barely had time to formulate the thought. There was a blur of movement on the edge of my field of vision.

Julia gave an ear-splitting shriek. She was pointing at the office building—not at the doors that Eddy was guarding but at another, smaller doorway about ten yards to the left.

There was Heinrich in his Balaclava.

Eddy swivelled round and fired.

CHAPTER FIFTEEN

Finch and Eddy had underestimated Heinrich. We all had. And in one way at least, he had underestimated us.

The echoes of the shot bounced around the yard.

Before the echoes had time to die away, I had most of it figured out. Heinrich had been a fool to leave the briefcase in Kinahan's office. It showed how confident he was. Okay, Finch and Eddy wouldn't have looked inside it on their own initiative and perhaps Heinrich felt he needed both hands free for the animal house. But he had failed to allow for the thousand-to-one chance. He'd failed to allow for our coming back for Gerald.

When he'd finished in the animal house, he must have returned to Kinahan's office to pick up the briefcase—and also, perhaps, to gloat at Gerald. Finch should have realized that the absence of both Gerald and the briefcase would make Heinrich instantly wary; that was *his* mistake. I had no reason to feel smug. I must admit that it hadn't occurred to me either. It would have done, maybe—if I'd had time to think things through. But, as I've said so often before, I didn't have time. None of us did.

So Heinrich had come cautiously and unexpectedly into the yard. Julia's shriek must have confirmed his suspicions—that and what Finch was doing and how Eddy reacted to seeing him. They'd left him in no doubt that his cover was blown.

All of this went through my mind at the speed of light. Through the back of my mind, as it were, not the front. It wasn't packaged in words and sentences: it was as if my brain had been injected with a dollop of pure knowledge in concentrated form.

Most of my attention was on the here and now. Things

113

were happening so fast that I could hardly untangle the sequence of events. Apart from me, everyone was moving.

As Eddy swivelled, he lost his balance. The shot he fired must have gone wide. His limbs thrashed as he tried to regain control. He fell sideways against the nearer of the technicians' cars.

Simultaneously, Finch went into a roll. He was a big, heavy man but he moved like a natural athlete. The roll ended with him lying on his stomach with his gun ready for use.

Cradling the briefcase, Smith flattened herself against the near side of the Land Rover, which meant that I was the only person who could see her. The Land Rover, of course, blocked her view of what was happening by the doors of the office building.

Over by the archway, Julia shook her fist and went on shrieking. "Traitor!" she yelled, which wasn't much help to anyone. The beagles who were near her caught the general idea and pranced around barking.

505 showed more sense. He cowered against my leg.

I expected Heinrich to duck back into the building. But he didn't. I suppose he was desperate, that he knew he had run out of options. Instead of retreating, he plunged towards Eddy.

Someone—Eddy or Finch or Heinrich?—fired another shot.

Eddy was trying to get up. Heinrich collided with him. They wriggled together. Eddy was on his knees with Heinrich stooping over him. It looked as if each was trying to get a grip on the other, each trying to avoid the other's gun. Finch couldn't fire for fear of hitting Eddy.

Suddenly Heinrich and Eddy were still. I was no more than twenty yards away so I had a good view. As far as I could see, neither of them had been hit by the bullet. Eddy's face was white, and he'd screwed up his features like a child does when it's on the verge of tears. Heinrich whispered something in his ear. Eddy's gun fell to the ground. Heinrich whispered another sweet nothing in his ear. Slowly, very slowly, Eddy stood up.

Heinrich had an armlock round Eddy's neck. He was using Eddy as a human shield. For a moment no one said a thing. Finch hadn't moved: he was still lying on his belly with his elbows on the ground and the gun trained on the two men in front of him.

Heinrich kicked Eddy's gun in a spray of gravel underneath the nearer of the cars. No doubt his own gun was boring into Eddy's back. It suddenly occurred to me that Heinrich didn't know that Smith and I were here. He probably thought Julia had freed Gerald. I could sidle down the steps and vanish. He wouldn't be any the wiser.

"Now be reasonable," Heinrich said.

"Let him go," Finch said. "Or I'll kill you."

"You'd kill us both." Heinrich glanced rapidly round the yard. "You don't want that."

"If *I* don't kill you – "

"Yes. Maybe the bomb will kill us all. Let's be pragmatic about this. We'll come to an arrangement. Much more sensible."

"I don't do deals with – "

"I just want to leave," Heinrich said. "I want the Land Rover and my briefcase with the contents intact. Then no one will get hurt."

Finch said nothing.

"Hurry. Time's getting on, isn't it? Put your gun on the ground and stand up."

"For God's sake, Finch," Eddy shouted. "Do as he says. It's our only chance."

"It's not just our baby," Heinrich went on. "The gardai must be on their way by now."

Finch lowered the gun. He laid it gently on the gravel. Heinrich ordered him to stand up and kick the gun into the open drain.

Everyone's attention was on Finch. Everyone except Smith, who was still holding the briefcase. I glanced at her. She stuck her left arm through the open window of the Land Rover. Then she straightened up and showed me what was in her hand: the keys.

I shook my head violently. I couldn't see any point in twisting Heinrich's tail. Smith obviously had other ideas. I didn't have a chance to argue with her. She lobbed the keys towards me. The gap between the Land Rover and the Nissan was in full view of the rest of the yard. The keys gleamed in a high, golden arc. No one noticed.

"Now stand where you are. That's it: where I can see you." I could hear the tension ebbing out of Heinrich's voice, which told me that Finch must have obeyed him. "And where have you put the briefcase?"

The keys jingled as I caught them with my left hand; I was holding the Zeiss with my other hand. I stuffed the keys in my pocket. 505 whined softly. I climbed a couple of steps. Smith poised herself on the balls of her feet, ready to make the dash towards me.

"By the Land Rover," Finch said.

"And the keys?"

"They're in the ignition."

Heinrich and Eddy had begun to move slowly towards the Land Rover. They looked like a bizarre animal with two heads and four legs: just the sort of nightmare creation you expect to find in an animal house.

I waved at Smith to run towards me. It was risky but her only chance. Heinrich was still looking at Finch, but in another moment he couldn't help but see her. I moved up the last few steps, ducking behind the burned-out shell of the Nissan. It wasn't the most logical thing to do but no one acts logically in a crisis. I had a confused and vaguely chivalrous idea that I'd be more use to Smith up there. I'd be able to cover her retreat. Or something like that.

The beagles went mad. Something white streaked across the yard from the archway. The dogs evaded Julia and hurtled after it. Julia hurtled after them, her arms outstretched. I grabbed 505's collar just in time to prevent him

116

from joining in the fun. The white streak zoomed under the Land Rover, braked sharply and turned into a white rat.

At the same time, Eddy tried to tear himself away from Heinrich. Finch dived towards the axe, which was lying on the ground a good ten yards away from him. Heinrich clubbed Eddy with the butt of his gun. I saw the blow descending but not where it landed: somewhere on the head or neck, I think. Eddy collapsed. Heinrich started running. He passed the Nissan and ran right round the Land Rover—down the offside and round the front to the nearside. If he'd looked to his right he would have seen me.

Instead he saw Smith.

Heinrich slowed to a walk. He smiled. Julia seized the collars of a couple of the dogs and dragged them away. The other beagles abandoned the rat and chased after Julia. Their barks had turned nasty. One of them leapt up and tried to bite her arm.

Heinrich was less than three yards away from Smith. "Put the briefcase in the Land Rover," he said.

Smith groped for the door handle. Heinrich swung his gun across the bonnet of the Land Rover. The barrel was in line with Finch, who by now was down on the ground with his hands on the axe.

"Back off," Heinrich ordered. And he turned sharply through ninety degrees, back to Smith. I knew exactly what he planned to do. It was as if I could see inside his mind.

He had nothing to lose by killing Smith, and quite a lot to gain. For one thing she was in his way; for another, her death would affect Astrid and, through her, Weyburn Cosmetics. And maybe he had a third reason, if that's the right word for it: a blind impulse to take revenge. Between us, Smith and I were responsible for ruining his evening.

I let go of 505 and straightened up. "Oy," I said. "You there."

The gun was still panning round. Smith's hand was on the door handle. Finch was scrambling up with the axe in his hand.

I threw the camera as hard and straight as I could. There was nothing else to do.

The Zeiss turned in the air. Its silver trim winked as it caught the light. Heinrich saw it coming. Automatically he raised his arm, his right arm, to ward it off.

The gun went off. The camera bounced off Heinrich's arm and hit the ground. 505 streaked along the Nissan, passed between Heinrich's legs and disappeared under the Land Rover. Heinrich, already off-balance, tripped over 505 and sat down heavily.

Smith ran. Not towards me or the archway, because Heinrich was in the way and he still had his gun. She swerved round the back of the Land Rover, to put it between her and Heinrich. She was still carrying the briefcase. I rounded the Nissan, stamped on Heinrich's left hand and ran after her.

The rat chose that moment to make a break for it. He shot across the yard towards the open doors of the office building. 505 went after him.

Finch was coming towards Smith and me. He was swinging the axe. I took it personally, and so did Smith— though with hindsight it was obvious that Finch was after Heinrich, not us.

We skirted Eddy, who was huddled on the gravel and moaning softly to himself. 505 followed the rat; Smith followed 505; and I followed Smith.

Heinrich fired once more. I didn't look round. We ran through the first set of doors and swept round the bend in the corridor. The carpet deadened the sound of our feet.

Finch hadn't got a gun, I thought; he wasn't a real threat to Heinrich even if the last bullet had missed. So why wasn't Heinrich pounding after us?

We came into the waiting room. The rat took cover under the sofa. And I had the answer to my question.

Heinrich didn't dare come after us. Because the bomb was just about to go off.

"The bomb!" I screamed.

Smith glanced at me. I saw blue eyes with sort of greeny flecks in them. I remember wondering if this was the last time I'd see them.

"They haven't come after us," I said. My head felt heavy and stupid. I looked down at the dog.

There wasn't much clearance between the sofa and the floor. 505 had stuck his nose in the gap at the front and was trying to squeeze underneath. The rat scuttled out at the back. It moved at speed along the line of the wall and made a right turn into the passage that led to the animal house. Heinrich had left one of the doors open.

"The bomb," Smith whispered.

She threw the briefcase into the secretary's room. It crashed into the VDU. The screen shattered. 505 dragged his head away from the sofa. He barked at me. I think he realized he'd been fooled and he expected me to do something about it.

So I followed the rat. Smith had had the same idea. We went through that door neck and neck, with 505 half a length behind.

In front of us the bleak corridor sloped down to the big double doors of the animal house. They were closed. The doors on the right, however, were wide open. A current of cool air flowed through them. 505 barked, this time with joy.

He'd seen not just one rat but a couple of dozen of them. They were outside on the path and the grass. Presumably they were still trying to make up their collective mind about how to cope with the freedom that Julia had thrust upon them.

119

505 accelerated the decision-making process. The rats scattered into the darkness. 505 ran outside. He nearly had a nervous breakdown trying to catch all of them at once.

I noticed all this because it filled my mind. I suppose it was a distraction. When you're lying in the dentist's chair, you make a map of an undiscovered world from the cracks in the ceiling. 505 and the rats were my map.

I lost sight of 505 and lost interest in him too. Smith grabbed my hand and we ran down the path. On our right were the two big windows of Kinahan's office. Inside, the timer on the bomb was still ticking away the seconds; outside, we were still in limbo.

I stumbled and almost fell. Smith stopped and yanked me up. We ran on. We reached the base of the terrace. All that solid masonry reared up like the wall of a castle. It sloped a few degrees away from the vertical.

Smith tugged my hand. She wanted to run down the overgrown lawn, away from Biercetown House. I remembered the force of the blast when the Nissan went up; and that had been a relatively small explosion.

"No," I gasped. "This way's safer."

So we ran along the path parallel to the terrace. If the terrace was a capital E, the path touched the tips of the three crossbars. We passed the first alcove; I glimpsed the door and two windows on the back wall. We passed the twin urns at the bottom of the flight of steps.

Once we were past the steps, I pulled Smith to the right. We swerved into the matching alcove on the far side of the steps. We went right to the end, to the left-hand corner.

Then, like the frightened animals we were, we went to ground. We put our arms around each other and made ourselves as small as possible. The grass was damp. On two sides we had the roughness of the terrace walls.

My back seemed terribly exposed. I felt the wind on my skin. It cooled the sweat that was streaming down my body. The air had a hint of rain in it. They say it always rains in Ireland.

I began to shiver. I couldn't stop trembling. Smith tightened her arms around me and I clung to her. She smelled of soot and sweat, petrol and perfume. Smells are very personal.

Someone's heart was thumping. Hers or mine or both? The beat grew louder and louder and faster and faster.

"Chris," Smith said, and I could hardly hear her for the roaring of the blood in my ears. "Chris? I want to tell you – "

I never heard the end of the sentence. She and I had left it too late to say all the things that needed to be said.

CHAPTER SEVENTEEN

My ears hurt. So did my shoulder. I think Smith had bitten the fleshy bit that runs above the collarbone.

I'd expected the initial noise of the explosion and the rush of displaced air. Everything else came as a surprise. I wasn't ready for the rumbles, the creaks and the crashes. I wasn't ready for the splintering of glass. I wasn't ready for the way the consequences seemed to last for ever.

Stones from the old house rained on to the terrace. As they thudded down, the retaining wall vibrated against my arm and the ground seemed to twitch in pain. Dogs barked and someone screamed. They sounded a long way away.

Everything was dark and the air was full of dust. I thought: *this is how the world will end.*

All the lights were out, even the security lamps that dotted the park. The explosion must have cut off the power supply. The dust made it hard to breathe. Grit caked my lips and blocked my nostrils; I could feel it on my tongue and on the roof of my mouth.

Smith's face was buried in my shoulder. She was crying, racking sobs that strained her lungs. It was odd: before the bomb went up, I was the one who was going to pieces; now our roles were reversed.

"Hush now," I said hoarsely. My voice sounded strange. Maybe something had happened to my eardrums.

We rocked to and fro. Gradually her sobs grew less violent. I was in a daze: my mind floated off. I wondered what had happened to all the other living things—to 505 and his mates, to the rats, the rabbits and the mice, to the two technicians, to Julia and Heinrich and Eddy and Finch. I'd forgotten someone. After a while I remembered who it was. Gerald was somewhere out there. Out of sight and almost out of mind.

I wondered what had happened to them but without much interest. It sounds awful, I know, but I really didn't give a damn. I was alive. Smith was alive. That was all I cared about. Fear makes you selfish, and so does relief. On the other hand I felt so grateful that we weren't dead that I wanted to thank someone.

"Do you think God exists?" I whispered. "If he does, I'd like to thank him."

Smith sniffed. "Or her." She gave a ghost of giggle. "Or it."

"Or a combination of all three." I coughed and spat out some grit. "Just to be on the safe side."

I looked up. It wasn't completely dark. The sky was a greyer shade of black. I thought I saw a star but when I looked again it had gone. The silence was uncanny. Even the dogs had stopped barking.

Smith snuggled closer to me. "I'm cold."

"So am I. It's weird."

I meant that it was weird to have enough leisure to talk about being cold. We seemed to have been running away for years.

"Is it over?"

"I think so," I said. "There's not much that Heinrich can do in the darkness. Or Finch."

"They may think we're dead. No one knows we're here."

"We're in limbo. We're – "

Gravel spattered on the path. Smith caught her breath. Something whined.

"Oh no," I said. "Here, boy."

A nose butted my leg. I stretched out my hand and felt a smooth head and two floppy ears.

"I don't think you've been introduced," I said to Smith. "This is probably 505."

I explained about the tag on the beagle's collar. 505 was

very pleased to find us. I was glad he was alive but less glad to have his company. Three's a crowd. 505 reminded me that we couldn't stay in our private limbo for the rest of our lives.

Perhaps Smith felt the same way. She pulled herself away from me. "I guess we should move."

"Why?"

"The cops will use the drive. We might as well be there to meet them."

"Might be better to stay where we are."

"Someone might need help."

I wasn't in a humanitarian mood. Just as I was about to say so, 505 stiffened. I grabbed his collar. He strained to get away. A second later we heard a pack of beagles in full cry somewhere on the other side of the animal house.

"Help!" Heinrich yelled in the distance.

And Finch was shouting too. I couldn't distinguish all the words but the general sense was clear enough. The dogs were pushing him right to the end of his tether.

The two of them were running away. The beagles had joined in, just for the fun of it. I doubted whether they'd be able to get out of the park. The sounds of the chase gradually decreased in volume.

"Hear that?" Smith said. "It's perfectly safe."

In a while the silence returned. Our eyes had adjusted to the darkness as much as they could. We got up and walked towards the end of the house—the opposite end from the yard. I glanced back but it was impossible to see what damage the bomb had done. I would have liked to take Smith's hand but I thought it might be pushing it; she might think I was taking an unfair advantage.

The path reached a T-junction at the end of the terrace. We turned right. We walked on the grass to avoid making unnecessary noise. 505 stayed close to us all the way. Rising gently, the path ran parallel to the side of the house. At the drive we stopped to listen.

Not very far away, someone was crying.

"Julia?" Smith called.

The crying stopped. Julia blundered towards us.

"Are you okay?" I said awkwardly.

"Everyone's gone. Oh God. I don't understand what happened."

"What about Eddy?" Smith said.

"He's no use," Julia wailed. "He's unconscious. The others just ran off. It shouldn't have happened like this, should it? If I'd known there'd be all this violence, all this mess . . ."

"You freed the animals," Smith said. "And after this, the Kinahans are going to have a lot of problems."

"And what are my parents going to say when – "

"Hey," I said. "Is the Land Rover still in the yard?"

Julia gulped in an affirmative sort of way.

"Here are the keys. Drive like hell and you might have a chance. Don't stop for the others, whatever you do."

She grabbed the keys. "Why are you doing this?" Her voice was heavy with suspicion.

"Don't waste time," I said.

"I can never understand people," Julia said. "They're too complicated. Animals are so much simpler."

She ran off—along the front of Biercetown House towards the archway to the yard. 505 went after her.

"Why did you do it?" Smith said.

"I don't know." My head filled with pictures: of Julia letting me escape because she was a little too decent to be ruthless; of her shooing the rats through a lighted doorway; of her saying *No one's going to get killed*. "She needed a break."

"It wasn't because you fancy her or something?"

"Are you joking?"

"Just asking."

505 came running back to us. He leaped up at me and then at Smith. He was acting as though he'd been away for years. I was glad of the interruption.

"Let's go back," Smith said abruptly. "Back to where we were."

I didn't know how she meant me to take the suggestion—literally or metaphorically. So I turned round and we walked back down the path. The Land Rover's engine fired and Julia drove away.

After a few paces I took Smith's hand. She didn't object.

"Why did you take the briefcase and keys?" I said. "You didn't need to."

Her fingers tightened on mine. "I just didn't want them to get away with everything."

"I thought you'd approve of some of what they were doing."

"If you must know," Smith said angrily, "maybe I did it for my mother too. Just a little."

The subject of Astrid is normally a minefield. I blundered into it. These were not normal circumstances.

"Has it worked?" I asked. "Seeing her again, I mean, after all these years?"

"No. We're total strangers. I don't even like her. That's the point. That's why I – "

She broke off, and nothing I could say would make her go on. I didn't press too hard. We got back to our alcove, and it felt a little like coming home. Smith let go of my hand. We sat down to wait for the Garda. 505 burrowed between us.

"I don't like what any of them are doing," Smith said. "My mother—Stephen Kinahan—Heinrich—Eddy and Finch. It all stinks. They all think the end justifies the means."

I tried to put my arm around her but she ducked away. I told myself it didn't mean anything. I think we were both feeling low. Sometimes it gets you that way when the tension relaxes.

The wind had died down. The hint of rain had turned into the real thing: a fine drizzle that chilled you to the bone. I thought I heard hammering in the distance. Maybe the Garda was trying to get in at one gate or Julia was trying to get out of the other.

"You know something?" I said. "I've missed Paul Anders yet again. I think I'm fated."

I was just trying to add a note of jollity to the occasion—to lighten the gloom a little. But I'd miscalculated.

"That's why you came to Dublin, isn't it?" Smith said. "The one goddamn reason. You wouldn't have come just to see me, would you?"

"Eh?" My mouth dropped open. No doubt I looked as stupid as I felt.

"You wouldn't even let me pay your air fare," she went on in a low, furious voice. "You didn't want to be under an obligation to me. Besides, that would have meant you'd have to spend longer with me, and that would never do. Oh no."

"Look," I said. "You've got this all wrong."

"I needed you. My mother was driving me crazy. I don't give a damn for Paul Anders."

"I didn't realize – "

"The English can't cope with the truth, can they? And shouting embarrasses them. They try to – "

I took a deep breath. "Stuff Paul Anders," I yelled. "I came to see *you*."

505 barked loudly. I pushed him out of the way.

"Now what about you and Gerald?" I said before Smith had a chance to recover. "You know, young love's dream."

"For God's sake," she snapped. "The guy gives me the creeps. I was trying to make you jealous. Trying to make you *do* something."

We were both shouting. Partly because we wanted to and partly because we needed to. The night was growing noisy. I could hear cars coming up the drive. A siren see-sawed in the distance. Overhead was the clatter of a helicopter, rapidly getting louder. The gardai were doing things in style. If Stephen Kinahan had got on to them when we failed to return from the Warehouse, they might suspect we'd be here.

"You stopped Heinrich killing me," Smith said.

"Maybe. I'd have done it for anyone."

Suddenly the world was unbearably bright. A searchlight cut down from the sky. The lawn glowed an unhealthy emerald green. The light tracked towards the terrace, missing us by inches, and blazed down on the house and the yard. 505 tried to bury himself underneath our bodies.

"You wrecked your camera."

"Yeah."

By now the rotors were making so much noise that we had our hands on each other's shoulders and our heads together. And we still had to yell to make ourselves heard.

"I'm going to buy you a new camera, okay? A better camera than you ever dreamed of getting."

"No, you're not," I said. "I pay my own way."

The helicopter touched down on the other side of the house. The rotors were still turning. Someone tried to make an announcement through a megaphone; but he had to give up because there was too much noise.

"I have never," Smith yelled, "in my entire life met anyone half as pigheaded as you."

"That makes two of us."

I grabbed her or maybe she grabbed me. In any case we rolled over on to the grass. We lay side by side and the gentle rain fell on top of us. The guy with the megaphone kept telling us we were surrounded. 505 licked Smith's hair, then mine. I wished they'd all go away and leave us alone in limbo. We squeezed the breath out of each other. Our mouths brushed together. We kissed.

"I love you," I said when I next had a chance to speak—just to put it on record: to avoid any misunderstandings in the future.

"Yeah," Smith said. "And I love you too."